HEAVY IRON

HEAVY IRON

Basil Copper

CHIVERS
THORNDIKE

This Large Print edition is published by BBC Audiobooks Ltd, Bath, England and by Thorndike Press®, Waterville, Maine, USA.

Published in 2003 in the U.K. by arrangement with the author.

Published in 2003 in the U.S. by arrangement with Basil Copper.

U.K. Hardcover ISBN 0–7540–7378–5 (Chivers Large Print)
U.K. Softcover   ISBN 0–7540–7379–3 (Camden Large Print)
U.S. Softcover   ISBN 0–7862–5841–1 (Nightingale)

The text of this Large Print edition is unabridged.
Other aspects of the book may vary from the original edition.

Set in 16 pt. New Times Roman.

Printed in Great Britain on acid-free paper.

British Library Cataloguing in Publication Data available

Library of Congress Control Number: 2003108164

CHAPTER ONE

1

'It looks like being a dry summer,' Manny Richter said.

I gave him one of my long glances, the forty-dollar kind, that would have been worth a fortune for close-ups in the movies. The forties sort, of course. They don't make them like that any more.

'It usually is,' I said.

Manny shifted his dead cigar from one side of his mouth to the other and cast a sad eye up at the fly-specks on the ceiling.

'I wasn't talking about the weather, Mike,' he said.

'You could have fooled me,' I told him.

He shrugged, his brown, seamed face burned with the Southern California sun of some fifty years giving him, for a brief moment, the look of a rock lizard. It was a likeness I'd often seen on the faces of characters in L.A. who literally didn't know enough to come in from the sun so that they finished up, in early middle-age, looking like a passport photo of Somerset Maugham in his dotage. Which was saying something.

But I was getting off the point. I'd dropped down to Manny's club this hot afternoon to make some inquiries about a client's financial standing and maybe follow up a couple of leads and stayed on to chew the fat for half an hour, which had lengthened to twice that.

The electric fan in the ceiling of Manny's office went on creaking in the turgid silence and the long, cool lime drink, the glass half-filled with crushed ice which Manny had ordered for me, kept me sitting on in the padded leather chair opposite his desk.

I didn't rise to Manny's bait so he had to break the silence first. He eased his bulk in his chair and squinted at me through the cloudy liquid in his glass. It was a French drink called pastis; I'd tried it once, long ago, before I'd learned you're supposed to dilute it with water. I felt it was an acquired taste.

Manny was a well-preserved character in his mid-sixties with a bald dome that glinted beneath the ceiling lights of his office and which made him look vaguely like Telly Savalas on his afternoon off. For the rest he had on a pearl-grey silk suit, a dazzling white shirt and a pale lemon yellow tie that was fixed in a tight knot beneath the shirt tabs. I couldn't have carried it off but it looked natty on him.

He'd been a New York boy until he was about sixteen or seventeen and had come out west to the coast; he'd fallen in love with it and had stayed on ever since, at first trying his hand at a little smuggling; then running a tuna-fishing operation and finally, as the result of

2

some unspecified deal which had turned him into a moderately well-heeled man, had bought his way into the L.A. nightclub circuit at a time when it was comparatively cheap to do so. Compared to today, of course.

From then on in he'd gone onward and upward; unlike many club owners he was absolutely on the square and I'd done a few discreet jobs for him from time to time, when he wanted things handled out of the public eye. Not that they were shady; Manny was a kind character and when a well-known senator's son welshed on his gambling debts or an upper-crust girl was behaving stupidly with a notorious hoodlum, he'd done his best to sort things out with a minimum of scandal.

Which was why I'd come here on such a torrid day, knowing I'd get a straight answer to a straight question. But Manny wasn't gabby at the best of times and I'd had to ask a lot of qualifying subsidiaries to elicit the information from his plain yes or no responses, which had taken an hour or so. I had the time, of course, so it didn't matter today; unlike some of my other assignments.

'Arid, perhaps,' he said at last.

I gave him another interrogative look.

'The weather?' I said.

He shook his head, his heavy sigh seeming to make a soft, moist explosion among the collection of spotlights that were suspended from the panelled ceiling.

His voice was so low I had to strain to hear his next comment.

'Cash-flow,' he said.

I eased forward in my chair and tapped my cigarette ash into the big copper tray on a corner of his desk.

'Oh, that.'

I grinned.

'I get it all the time. It's an occupational hazard in my business. Sometimes the clients get killed and then I don't get paid at all.'

Manny looked at me blandly.

'But you do come out alive, Mike.'

'Generally,' I told him.

We were getting off the subject.

'What have cash-flow problems to do with the night club business?' I said. 'I thought lots of greenbacks pass all the time. The business is strictly cash if my paperback thrillers have it right.'

Manny Richter closed one eye in a movement that could have been a wink or a sudden nervous tic. It was sometimes difficult to tell with men of his age.

'In general, yes. But we have suppliers, business associates, chains of people who both receive money from us and owe as well. I have an interest in six or seven clubs, as well as other enterprises. The Blue Moon is my favourite. Which is why I make it my headquarters.'

'You don't have to draw a picture,' I said.

4

Manny Richter shrugged, leaning forward to put the well-worn elbows of his suit on the polished leather surface of his desk. His eyes were so far closed now that the whites showed as mere strips of light beneath his heavy lids. The simile of a rock lizard was stronger than ever.

'There's some sort of gang-war going on, Mike,' he said deliberately. 'It's affecting my sort of business particularly.'

'That stuff went out years ago,' I said.

Manny shook his head.

'It's a little more subtle than that, Mike. Though crude in its outward manifestations.'

He looked at me grimly.

'Don't you read the papers?' he asked after a long silence. 'I'm talking about the Tattoo Murders.'

2

I leaned forward and took another long sip of my drink. The casual movement seemed to irritate him suddenly.

'Seems like you don't know much about it.'

I shook my head.

'Never heard of them,' I told him.

Manny stared at me incredulously. I went on before he could break in.

'I've been away on vacation for three weeks. Up around San Francisco.'

Richter grunted, again shifting in his chair.

'Four in the last month,' he said. 'Murders, mean. All males, all with tattoo markings on them.'

'Sounds interesting,' I said. 'But I can't see how it would concern you. Personally, I mean.'

Manny gave me a hurt look.

'One of them was a man who owed me a lot of money, Mike,' he said in a low voice. 'Upwards of fifty thousand dollars. I was sorry about him, of course.'

He gave a crooked shrug, a wry look on his face now.

'I feel sorrier for myself.'

'Naturally,' I said. 'You're not asking me to look into this for you? The boys in blue would have picked up all the pieces.'

Richter shook his head.

'I'm not asking you to do anything, Mike. Except keep your eyes and ears open. If you hear anything that might lead me in the direction of my money I'd be obliged if you'd tip me off.'

I leaned over and stubbed out my cigarette butt in his tray, then sat back and toyed with my drink again. There was no sound in the office now except for the faintest perceptible hum of the air-conditioning and the squeak of the fan. I wondered why he needed both.

'Sure I will,' I said.

Manny's eyes were mocking now.

'Except that you were up in San Francisco and hadn't heard a thing about it.'

He reached across the desk and came up with a crumpled copy of the *Examiner*. He threw it across towards me. I caught it when it was about a foot from the floor, straightened it out. Manny watched me unblinkingly.

'Right-hand page lead,' he said. 'There's a resumé of the three kills in the centre-spread. When you've boned up on things you might let me have your opinion. Jerry Freeman's my man.'

I nodded, scanning the heavy type headlines. Like Manny said it was a gift for the more sensational sheets. The *Examiner* was pretty staid as newspapers go but even they'd opened up a little.

'What about his family?' I said. 'Any chance of collecting from them. You got something in writing, I take it?'

Manny nodded gloomily.

'Sure, Mike. I'm a businessman. But you ought to know you can't collect on a dead man. It cancels out.'

'It cancels out a lot of things,' I said.

I sat and sipped my drink. There seemed to be a lot of unspoken thoughts hanging in the air between us.

'You might look into it, Mike,' Manny Richter said gently. 'On an informal basis, of course. And without mentioning my name.'

'I'll let you know if I hear anything,' I said.

The big club owner nodded reflectively. 'That's fair enough,' he said gently.

7

I guessed the loss of his fifty thousand greenbacks must have been affecting him plenty. I'd never heard him so gabby before.

'You mentioned in these stories?' I said.

Manny shook his head.

'Nothing like that. But I hear around town that Jerry owed big. Maybe that was why he was killed.'

'Sounds a screwy way of debt collecting,' I said. 'You think the other two owed money as well?'

Manny gave another shrug.

'Who knows? If I was a dick I'd be more interested in the tattoo marks.'

'Maybe,' I said. 'Except that I haven't had a chance to read things up.'

'Sure,' Manny said. 'You were on vacation.'

I rose, finished off my drink and we shook hands. There didn't seem to be anything else to say. Manny stopped me as I got up near the door.

'Freeman had a nice wife,' he said. 'Girl named Deirdre. You might start with her. The *Examiner* gives the address.'

I stared at him for a long moment, not seeing the claustrophobic walls of his office.

'I'll think about it,' I said.

The smog and the fumes of L.A. seemed almost like the fresh air of the countryside when I got back on the street.

CHAPTER TWO

1

I put the *Examiner* down on my desk and squinted at Stella through the haze of smoky sunshine that spilled in through the window blinds. Today she wore a white silk dress with a faint zig-zag blue pattern running through it that fitted her like a second skin. It seemed to ripple and undulate every time she walked and it was putting me off the prospects of my coffee.

If you know what I mean. She smiled at me like she knew what I was thinking and went over to the glassed-in alcove where we do the brewing-up, with a rat-tatting of heels that increased my blood count.

But it was too hot for all that sort of stuff this afternoon and I settled back at my old broadtop and squinted at the cracks in the ceiling like they might hold the answer to Manny Richter's problem. I sighed and smoothed out the *Examiner* again.

The item Manny was so stirred up over was downpage but it still rated heavy headlines. THIRD RED DRAGON MURDER the main streamer blared. And underneath, in slightly smaller type; No Clues in Latest Tattoo Slaying.

I went down the columns again. I had the salient points. Manny's client, Jerry Freeman, was the third in the series. That was the character who owed him all the money, according to Manny. He'd asked me about the wife. I might go see her.

The business was nothing to do with me and there wasn't even a case in it but I owed him a favour or two and he'd been pretty co-operative today.

Stella came back while I was running down the resumé of the kills that a by-lined staffer had dug out the files and had the subs put in a box to run alongside the main story. I reached over and tore off the entire sheet and then the turn on the back page. Stella sat down on the edge of my desk and cupped two pink-nailed hands around a smooth brown knee. It was her left, perhaps the best, and it was already doing something to my reflexes.

I shifted in my swivel chair and tried to avoid the innocent stare of those very blue eyes. The blonde bell of Stella's hair shimmered beneath the overhead lamp as she shifted position too.

'There's nothing in it for you, Mike,' she said.

I shrugged.

'Maybe not, honey. But I more or less promised Manny I'd try and see whether some of his money might be recoverable.'

Stella frowned, tossing her head with a little

10

impatient gesture.

'You can't collect from the dead, Mike,' she said.

I stared beyond her to where the fouled-up traffic belched fumes into the vibrating air of the boulevard.

'I know all that,' I said. 'I'm trying to do Manny a favour.'

Stella smiled. I could have watched it all day. Then she slipped off the desk with a rippling movement and went briskly back to the alcove. I sat savouring the aroma of freshly roasted beans and went through the Red Dragon slayings for the third time.

The press had labelled them like that because each of the men carried a small red dragon tattoo on their right arm up near the shoulder.

'If they'd been Chinese and young it might have been a tong war,' Stella said.

I moved my chair so that I could see her slim shadow moving against the glass.

'We already went into that,' I said. 'They were all white and various ages.'

Stella came back and put my filled cup down on the blotter, skipped out before I could grab her. Her smile lasted me all the way into my second cup. She came back with her own and the biscuit tin and sat down in the client's chair opposite and looked at me gravely. The pecking of the plastic-bladed fan went on eroding the blurred edges of the

11

silence. Like always the air-conditioning in our building wasn't working.

'So what then.'

I gave her one of my reflective stares through the blue smoke of the cigarette I'd just lit.

'Homosexuals, maybe,' I said. 'They go in for tattooing and all that sort of stuff, I understand.'

Stella raised her eyebrows and gave a little shiver of distaste.

'I know, honey,' I said. 'It isn't your scene. But it's the world we live in.'

She smiled faintly.

'You're stealing my lines,' she said. 'Jerry Freeman was married anyway.'

'That doesn't invalidate my point,' I said. 'Let's just run through the set-up. After you've passed me the biscuits, of course.'

2

I bit into the second of my butter-nut fudge specials in the cloying silence. Stella sat the other side of the desk and tapped her gold pencil against very white teeth.

'The only thing linking the four kills is the similarity of the tattoo marks,' I said. 'The police have established the tattoos were either done in some other part of the States or carried out privately.'

Stella raised her eyebrows.

'Meaning what?'

I shrugged.

'I don't know much about these things. Apparently something about the dyes used in the tattoos. They were special and had an unusual shade. Which let out all the tattoo parlors in the L.A. area.'

Stella gave me a very bright smile.

'It saved you some footwork, Mike.'

'I'm not on this case,' I reminded her. 'It isn't murder. I'm trying to recover some money on behalf of Richter, remember?'

'I remember,' Stella said.

But she still went on smiling anyway.

'Four kills in a month,' I said. 'All male; the first aged thirty-six; the second sixty-four; the third thirty-two; the fourth fifty-eight.'

'The third being Jerry Freeman,' Stella said.

I nodded, feathering out blue smoke at the ceiling.

'Just as Richter was about to hit him for 50,000 bucks he owed,' I said.

Stella made a wry mouth.

'Convenient.'

'You could say that,' I said.

'Maybe he owed money all over,' Stella said. 'And someone got tired of waiting.'

I stared at her in silence for a moment.

'Maybe. But it doesn't really add up. Characters who are owed that sort of dough would rather have the cash. And all the while the guy's alive they have a chance of

13

collecting.'

I flipped over the *Examiner* again.

'Each man killed with a .38 bullet in the back of the head,' I said. 'The first two and the last with the same gun.'

Stella took another sip at her coffee. She scribbled a fresh note on her pad and reached out for the biscuit tin.

'Which could or could not be significant,' she reminded me.

'Point taken,' I said.

She got up and went over to her own desk for a street directory. She came back, wrote something down and tore off the sheet. She passed it across the blotter to me.

'That's the widow's address,' she said. 'I take it you'll go see her after you've finished your coffee.'

I sighed.

'It was so nice sitting here chewing the fat like this.'

Stella smiled one of her long, lazy smiles.

'But it doesn't pay the bills, Mike.'

She had a point there. I never argue with things like that. I picked up the newspaper again and went down the columns once more.

'I'll make notes of the relevant detail and type them up when you've gone,' Stella promised me.

I grinned at her through the ascending smoke whorls of my cigarette.

'Slave-driver.'

14

'There's another interesting point, Mike,' Stella went on after a moment or two.

'The first two kills and the fourth took place in the men's apartments. That of Jerry Freeman was in a car.'

'I had noticed,' I said mildly. 'The hire-car was parked off one of the main boulevards late at night. He was at the wheel and had been neatly shot in the back of the head. Death had occurred about five hours before the body was found.'

Stella frowned. It didn't affect her beauty any.

'Does that say anything to you, Mike?'

I frowned back.

'Not much except that there are a lot of violent characters around L.A.'

Stella gave me one of her long-suffering looks.

'He was shot while he was in the driving seat. That meant the killer had to be in the rear section of the automobile.'

'I should have thought that was fairly obvious, honey,' I said.

Stella raised her eyes to the cracks in the ceiling, kept them there for a long time.

'Don't overstrain your brain,' I said. 'Come to the point.'

Stella's eyes were deceptively mild.

'It's just a detail, Mike,' she said patiently. 'Maybe Jerry Freeman was driven there at gunpoint. Or there might be something else.'

15

'Like what?' I said.

'Like this,' Stella said. 'He could have been shot by his passenger. Someone he knew and trusted.'

There was a long silence in the office, broken only by the faint whine of a bluebottle trapped between the window blind and the glass. I went over and let him out into the smog of L.A. He didn't even give me a backward glance.

I remained at the window, looking down at the seething mass of metal on the boulevard, not really seeing it.

'I'll think about it,' I told Stella in the end.

She was back at her own desk now, checking her notes.

'In the meantime you'd better drag your underwear over in the direction of La Brea,' she said. 'I'm part of the team. And I like to eat too.'

I didn't argue with her. I went on out before she could come up with anything else.

CHAPTER THREE

1

Jerry Freeman's place was a nice, architect-designed spread in the Bauhaus style set in about two acres of shaved turf, tropical vegetation and flowering trees. It took me about an hour to get across there and the shadows were stencilled long and heavy on the ground as I tooled my five-year-old powder-blue Buick up the red gravel driveway and parked in front of a weathered stone fountain that was doing its best to make Southern California look like Siena.

Or something about that price-range. I got out the Buick and slammed the driving door, the sound making a mournful echo across the fretting noise the palms were making in the light breeze that had sprung up here. I went on across the driveway to the imposing white bulk of the house, my thoughts heavy as my size nines on the concrete tiling as I got up in the colonnaded porch. I was wearing one of my semi-tropical suits but I could feel a patch of sweat forming in the small of my back already.

The heat of the day was still bouncing off the facade of the house but it was cool in the porch and I lingered for a moment, grateful for the shade after the stifling drive up. I wasn't looking forward to the interview. I'm not much good with widows and I hoped Jerry Freeman's wouldn't be the young, hysterical kind.

I knew Freeman had been in oil; Manny Richter had told me. This spread was that of a rich man. So what was a character like him doing borrowing money from Manny in the first place? Something here didn't sit right. But

17

I wouldn't find out what it was by hanging around so I went on over to the big front door, which was standing ajar; held back by a heavy bronze ornament, to let the breeze penetrate to the shadowy hall beyond.

That was something I hadn't taken up with Manny. Stella was right though. I was here to try and collect Manny's fifty thousand dollars, not to investigate the tattoo murders; the police had them well in hand. But Stella's suggestions had thrown up a lot of interesting possibilities and the more I mulled them around in what was left of my brain, the more intrigued I became.

I pressed the bell-button that was set in a solid brass surround to one side of the doorway and heard its sonorous pealing somewhere back in the house. You're becoming a regular Emily Dickinson again, Mike, I told myself. I waited for perhaps two minutes, my eyes slowly adjusting to the lowered intensity of lighting in the hall.

I saw a polished parquet floor; white walls; plenty of very expensive-looking oils in equally expensive gold frames; and a mahogany spiral staircase snaking up at the right-hand side of the hallway. It looked an antique; like something one would see in a baroque mansion in Austria or Middle Europe and I guessed it had been imported.

But I didn't have time to do any more inventory work because there came the high

18

staccato of a woman's heels on the parquet and a Filipino maid, good-looking, with lots of white teeth and dressed in a very chic black and white maid's outfit came waltzing across from a door set in the far wall.

As she came closer I saw that her eyes were swollen and red like she'd been crying.

'Yes?'

The voice was dead and non-committal.

'I'd like to see Mrs Freeman if it's possible,' I said.

The girl's white face beneath the shining black hair seemed blank and frozen now.

'You know what's happened?'

I hesitated. Then I made my voice as gentle as possible.

'Yes. I wanted to talk to Mrs Freeman about her husband if she'll see me.'

The girl kept her eyes averted, her gaze focused somewhere on the mellow sun-dazzle of the porch behind me. Then she seemed to recollect herself. There was momentary alarm in her voice as she looked squarely at me for the first time.

'You're not from the press?'

I shook my head.

'Cross my heart.'

The faintest of smiles lifted the corners of the girl's mouth. It completely transformed her face.

'She's had a terrible time with the press.'

I nodded.

'I can imagine. My name's Faraday. She wouldn't know me but I'd appreciate it if she'd see me for a few minutes.'

The girl made a vague inclination of the head as though she were thinking deeply about my request.

'Come in, Mr Faraday,' she said at last.

'I'll go find out.'

I walked into the hallway and she closed the big door behind me, sliding the bronze across the floor with a low slithering sound. The echo of the door slamming sounded like an explosion that started other echoes up and down the staircase.

'You care to tell me your business, Mr Faraday?'

I shook my head.

'It's confidential. I don't think she'd like it known.'

The girl's startled eyes were momentarily raised to mine. I forestalled her next question.

'I won't upset her,' I said. 'And I promise you I'll leave quietly.'

The maid smiled again. Then she went back out through the same door she'd come in, looking like an insubstantial shadow in the dimness, leaving me to my thoughts and the heavy pumping of my heart.

2

She was back within five minutes, looking

more brisk and cheerful.

'Mrs Freeman will see you, Mr Faraday,' she said, like she was conferring some great benefit. 'I'll show you up.'

I followed her across the parquet. When we were halfway she turned, looking at me sidewise from beneath long eyelashes.

'My name's Adele,' she said inconsequentially.

She put a slender, pink-nailed finger on my arm.

'Confidentially, Mr Faraday, Mrs Freeman is in a bad way. She's been sedated so she may appear somewhat sluggish in her reactions.'

She looked at me frankly, her eyes wide.

'I thought you ought to know that.'

'Sure,' I said. 'I understand. And I promise not to tire her.'

The girl went on without speaking, walking fast now like she'd made up her mind about something. She paused again as she got to the far door, one hand on the heavy antique brass knob.

'Only fifteen minutes if you please, Mr Faraday,' she said gently. 'The doctor said Mrs Freeman shouldn't talk too much in her present state of mind.'

'Devoted couple were they?' I said.

I was talking about Mrs Freeman and the murdered man, of course. Adele's brown eyes were clouded with reminiscence.

'I never saw such devotion, Mr Faraday. It's something you don't find very often.'

21

'You can say that again,' I said.

The girl opened the door and stood aside for me to precede her. I waited while she closed it behind us.

We were in a high, bright room now, that was got up like a study. I guessed it belonged to the late Freeman because the books, so far as I could make out in the short time available, were mostly on company law, the oil industry and other technical matters.

The girl had noticed my glances and she fixed my eyes with hers in one of her rare direct looks.

'We're going to the sun-room, Mr Faraday. It was their favourite place for sitting and enjoying drinks in the early evening.'

I shook my head.

'You think it's a good thing for her to sit there now. Under the circumstances, I mean?'

The maid shrugged.

'Who knows what's in another person's mind, Mr Faraday. It seems to give her comfort and that's the main thing.'

'I won't argue with that,' I said.

We were up in front of a pair of big glass doors set in teak frames that made a sort of mediaeval framework at the far end of the library. Beyond it I could see a lush world of tropical plants; a polished tile floor; and, still farther off, the green coolness of the garden shot through with mellow bars of sunlight. It was like something out of The House

22

Beautiful.

The girl opened one of the side wings now and I stepped through into paradise lost.

3

The woman who rose somewhat unsteadily from a long cane chair at the far end of the conservatory wasn't at all what I had expected. Though she showed obvious signs of the strains and grief that had marked her features in the past weeks she was far from the drugged, semi-comatose invalid my conversation with the maid had prepared me for.

She was about twenty-eight years old, I should have said; tall and willowy with that athletic figure one had grown familiar with from the work of English actresses in old American movies on TV. She had long blonde hair that fell forward in elegant sweeps across her eyes; for the rest the forehead was smooth and broad, the lips full and sensual with little lines of humour at the corners.

Her cheeks were pale, of course; that was only to be expected; the green eyes were dull where one would expect them to be sparkling; and there were dark stains beneath them which indicated sleepless nights.

But her manner was animated enough as she came slowly toward me, extending a small brown hand for me to shake.

'Mr Faraday?' she said hesitantly. 'I believe that was the name Adele said.'

She waved me to another cane chair, a tall, straight-backed one this time which stood opposite hers, with a low coffee table in between.

'But I can't recall . . .'

'You wouldn't know me, Mrs Freeman,' I interrupted quickly. 'And it was good of you to see me. I appreciate it at such a time. Would it do any good if I said how sorry I am. About your husband, I mean.'

The girl bit her lip, turning her eyes down to the black and white tiled floor.

'No good at all, Mr Faraday. But I'm grateful for the thought. Will you stay for tea? We're just going to have some.'

'If you're sure it's all right,' I said.

The Freeman girl smiled bitterly.

'What else would I do with myself now?' she said. 'I have all the time in the world.'

I sat down like she said. There didn't seem to be any answer to that. Mrs Freeman went vaguely toward the bank of greenery at the rear of the conservatory, then came quickly back as though she had recollected herself.

She was wearing white tennis shorts with white flat shoes and silk matching socks; and her white silk blouse, open at the throat, showed a discreet gold locket chain in the vee of the neck. For the rest she wore a plain gold wedding ring and gold watch on her left wrist.

Like everything else about her it was simple but denoted quality.

She sat down with an effort, gathering up her nerve-ends with difficulty and looked at me intently.

'Adele said you weren't a journalist . . . I couldn't bear that.'

I shook my head.

'Neither could I, Mrs Freeman. I don't like them either. Though there are a few good ones around.'

'Call me Deirdre,' the girl said irrelevantly. 'All my friends do. We're very informal here.'

She looked up as the shadow of the Filipino girl passed across the densely packed green fronds that made a shadowy place of the great domed building. We sat in sunlight at the front, overlooking the grounds, but the doors were open there, letting in a welcome breeze.

'We'll have tea now, Adele,' Deirdre Freeman said. 'Mr Faraday is staying.'

The dark girl shot me a quick smile like I'd met with her approval.

'Very well, Mrs Freeman.'

She glided out so quickly I couldn't catch her exit. I looked at Deirdre Freeman searchingly.

'I wouldn't want to be here under false pretences,' I said. 'But it's rather a delicate matter. I don't think this is really the time.'

The girl's eyes were alert now. She glanced at me with a quickening of interest.

25

'It's about my husband?'

'Sort of,' I said. 'Not about his death.'

I looked away from her to where the fading flare of the sun turned the lawns and shrubbery to a pale buttermilk colour.

'I'm an acquaintance of Manny Richter,' I said. 'He knew your husband too.'

Deirdre Freeman leaned back on the cushions of the cane chair and frowned at her finger-nails.

'I've heard the name, Mr Faraday. Jerry had many friends and business associates.'

'Richter owns a club the other side of town,' I said. 'You probably know it. The Blue Moon.'

I waited for a reaction but nothing was forthcoming. Deirdre Freeman reached for a pair of dark glasses that were lying on a corner of the coffee table and put them on, as though suddenly aware that her eyes showed traces of her sleepless nights. She stared at me over the dark cheaters.

'I know it,' she said in a low, well-modulated voice. She had the faintest trace of an English accent now that I came to think of it.

'It appears that your husband owed Mr Richter some money,' I said. 'This is only an informal approach, you understand. But he wanted me to ask if there was any chance the amount might be settled.'

The girl stirred impatiently in the chair, throwing her long golden hair back from her

26

eyes. She gave another of her bitter smiles.

'So you're nothing but a bill collector, Mr Faraday?'

I shook my head, giving her my own twisted smile in return.

'Not exactly,' I said. 'And I don't make a habit of pestering lovely ladies for money when their husbands have just been murdered.'

The girl leaned forward and reached for a pack of cigarettes and a lighter on the table. She lit one and puffed out smoke with quick, jerky exhalations of breath.

'It doesn't look like it from where I'm sitting,' she said in a chintzy voice. 'How much was Jerry supposed to owe this Mr Richter?'

'He mentioned fifty thousand dollars,' I said.

The girl inclined her head.

'Doesn't he know that debts die with the debtor?' she said.

'I told him that,' I said. 'He left it to your sense of fair play.'

The blonde number smiled genuinely this time.

'A club owner with a sense of humour,' she told the palm fronds.

'You could call it that,' I said.

The girl slowly removed the dark cheaters, leaned forward in the chair and examined my face searchingly.

'And what would my husband be doing

borrowing money from a club owner? He's worth a great deal.'

I shrugged.

'Manny didn't say. But he has lots of business interests. He owns a piece of a race-track at Santa Monica and he's generally into horses and gambling.'

The girl's mouth curved in a mocking smile.

'I see. Yes, it would be quite possible, Mr Faraday.'

She leaned forward again, holding my glance for a long time.

'Just exactly who are you?'

'I'm a private detective,' I said.

CHAPTER FOUR

1

The uneasy silence was broken by the clatter of the Filipino girl's heels coming back. Deirdre Freeman discontinued her baffled look and became the gracious hostess, fussing around with stuff on a silver tray. From the expression on the maid's face I gathered that she approved of my being there. At least it gave her mistress something to do instead of the endless hours she'd probably spent staring out across the garden.

She withdrew quietly and left us to the

toasted teacakes and the dainty little sandwiches that she'd cooked up.

'I hope you like China tea, Mr Faraday.'

'It's an acquired taste,' I said. 'But I have been known to imbibe from time to time.'

The girl gave a little tinkling laugh which seemed to echo uneasily among the acres of glass in here.

'What's so amusing?' I said.

She leaned forward to hand me a fragile-looking cup which had tropical birds painted in delicate lines upon it.

'You're a strange man, Mr Faraday. You breeze in here to disturb my mourning. You make a point of saying you're not a snooping reporter and then you calmly try to put the bite on me for fifty thousand dollars. On top of everything else you're a private eye. Did Mr Richter expect me to use physical violence in resisting his claims?'

I leaned forward and put the cup down on the coffee table gently.

'That's unfair,' I said. 'It was nothing like that at all.'

'What would you call it?' she said quickly.

I didn't attempt to answer.

'I was merely making some inquiries for a client at Manny Richter's place. He mentioned a series of murders. I'd never heard of them. I'd been out of town on vacation.'

There was a flush on the girl's cheeks now.

'Do go on, Mr Faraday,' she said in a calmer

voice.

I reached out and took another sandwich at her nodded invitation. They were pretty good but I hadn't come here for the social notes.

'He said something about your husband owing him this money. I told him the debt would be cancelled. I also felt it seemed unlikely such a rich man would want to borrow such a relatively small sum from a character like him.'

There was genuine humour in the girl's faint smile.

'Perfectly correct, Mr Faraday. But I have the answer to that in a moment. Why did you decide to come?'

I shrugged.

'Curiosity, maybe. I'd promised Manny I'd find out the situation informally. But I read up the cases in the papers this morning. I'd like to help, if I could. Like I said, I'm not a debt collector. I'll tell Manny he can go whistle for his money.'

The girl reached forward to pick up my cup, poured me another. Her eyes, without the dark cheaters, were wide and clear now. She gave me a brief, hesitant smile.

'I'll settle with Mr Richter,' she said calmly. 'You can tell him to let me have something in writing and I'll send a cheque in return.'

'You don't have to,' I said.

She handed me the cup, her fingers warm as they made fleeting contact with mine against

30

the saucer.

'I know that, Mr Faraday. But I'm settling all outstanding debts of that sort. There were quite a few.'

I shook my head.

'I don't get it, Mrs Freeman.'

'Deirdre,' she corrected me.

'My name's Mike,' I said. 'The bills, I mean. Your husband was a rich man.'

The girl flung the hair back from her eyes again in a gesture with which I was becoming familiar.

'It was Jerry's Achilles heel. It was the only thing we quarrelled over. He was an insatiable gambler. He would have wagered his entire fortune on the turn of a card or the nose of a pony. I had to take legal precautions. All company avenues were closed to him, except for legitimate expenditure.'

She smiled wryly.

'I almost left him once. He was broken up and we came to an agreement. I even monitored and added up his cheque stubs. We had joint accounts in various banks and we had arrangements with them to inform me of any irregularity.'

She made a strange little gesture of the hand in the air between us.

'It was degrading but it was the only way. I knew it wouldn't stop him, of course. It was a disease, like alcohol. So he ran up accounts with various friends and business acquaintances.

Every so often he'd confess and I'd have to pick up the tabs. But it was better than him selling out everything we'd built up on the turn of a card.'

I thanked her for the tea and got up to go when she stopped me with a swift gesture of the hand.

'Please stay, Mike. There are more important things than money. I'd like to talk to you seriously.'

2

I grinned.

'I thought we had been talking seriously.'

She shook her head, moving to re-fill my tea cup.

'I want the man or men who killed my husband found. I want them to rot in gaol for the rest of their lives.'

'It's a big order,' I said. 'The police haven't come up with anything yet.'

The girl made an impatient movement of her shoulders. A shaft of sunlight coming in through the open doors stained her pale cheeks until she looked like a bronze statue. I thought I hadn't seen anything more beautiful all month.

'The police know more than they've told the press.'

'What makes you say that?' I said.

Deirdre Freeman's eyes were smouldering.

'That was a beastly think to put out,' she said. 'They have no proof of anything like that.'

'You mean some sort of homosexual society?' I said.

Deidre's cheeks were dark red and she kept her eyes averted.

'I would sue the scandal sheet over that awful smear if I thought it would do any good.'

'Homosexuals do go in for tattoos a good deal,' I said. 'It's like a badge of membership. It's obvious that your husband didn't know the other three victims?'

The girl shook her head.

'The whole idea is ridiculous in Jerry's case. I would have known even if such things weren't absolutely abhorrent to him.'

The light smile was back on her lips.

'He was the original WASP.'

'All right,' I said. 'So maybe he had the tattoo done in a fit of youthful enthusiasm while serving in the Armed Forces.'

Deirdre Freeman shook her head vehemently.

'That's the strange part. He never had that tattoo on his arm from the time I first met him or during the whole of our married life.'

There was a long silence between us. I looked at her incredulously.

'I'm afraid I don't follow.'

The blonde girl traced the line of the tiling at her feet with a white shoe.

33

'I hadn't seen Jerry for three months. He was on a tour of the Far East drumming up business. Maybe he had it done out there.'

I kept my eyes on her face.

'Maybe,' I said.

The girl went on quickly, like she wanted to unburden herself.

'Jerry was on his way home that night. He was driving a hire-car when somebody put that bullet in him from behind. So I never did get to see him again.'

I kept my head down on my cup as I added a mite more sugar to my tea. I reached out for another of the tea-cakes while the girl recovered herself.

'So you're telling me all this Red Dragon stuff is just coincidence,' I said.

Deirdre Freeman put down her cup in the saucer with a faint chinking sound.

'I don't know, Mike,' she said wearily. 'I've been going over it again and again in my mind.'

'The Chinese go in for red dragons,' I said. 'And he'd just been out East.'

The girl looked up eagerly.

'You have some ideas?'

'Maybe,' I said cautiously. 'There are a number of things that could stand looking into.'

'Like a fifth one,' she said.

'Fifth what?' I said.

The girl looked at me with narrowed eyes.

'Tattoo murder,' she said. 'A flash came

over the radio just before you came. Which was why I was so upset when Adele came to announce you. A prominent L.A. TV producer named Petty. He was in his forties.'

I nodded slowly.

'Like I said there are some things about the situation that could stand looking into.'

The girl got up and walked over toward me. She was taller than I remembered and she seemed incredibly remote and far away as she stared down at me.

'You can tell your Mr Richter everything will be taken care of, Mike. And I want you to do me a favour in return.'

I already knew what it was even before she opened her mouth again.

'I'm pretty busy right now,' I lied.

She shook her head.

'You're not busy at all. I can always tell when people aren't speaking the truth. The intonation isn't right. And if you are, drop your other cases.'

'You haven't seen my licence yet,' I said lamely.

It was her turn to smile.

'I don't have to. As soon as you mentioned your Christian name I realised where I'd heard it before. You're well-known around L.A. And you're one of the best in the line.'

'I'd better add your testimonial to my box in the *Examiner*,' I said.

She brushed aside my feeble crack.

'Will you find Jerry's murderer for me?' she breathed.

I got up then, too conscious of those shapely brown legs in the white shorts that trembled slightly at my eye-level. I found I could just gaze down into her eyes. She was exactly the right height for me.

'I'll give it a whirl, Deirdre,' I said.

CHAPTER FIVE

1

Deirdre Freeman's three-thousand dollar retainer seemed to burn a hole in my wallet as I walked back across the hall. Another hour had gone by and we'd chewed the fat a while longer but nothing more illuminating than what I'd already picked up had emerged. I hadn't wanted the commission; hadn't asked for it, but something had been nudging me toward it ever since Manny Richter's veiled suggestion in his office.

I couldn't deny I was interested in the subject. It was like something out of a Perry Mason novel. I didn't think they came like that any more. Dragon tattoos on the victims were somehow too colourful and tell-tale for crime in the late twentieth century.

Not that I could have turned down Deirdre

Freeman anyway. I was imagining the quizzical look in Stella's eyes when I told her about our new client.

I was so absorbed in my thoughts I hardly noticed the slender form of the dark Filipino girl emerge from the shadows at the foot of the spiral staircase.

'Mr Faraday?'

The girl's eyes were flickering with strange lights as she faced me near the doorway through which I'd come in.

'Would you do me a favour?' I shrugged.

'That depends what it is.'

The maid had her eyes down on her feet again now. She seemed pretty good at that.

'Would you keep me informed of your progress on this case.'

'What case?' I said.

The dark girl gave me a long, sleepy smile.

'Mrs Freeman asked you to find who killed her husband, didn't she?'

I gave her one of my steady looks.

'I don't see that's any business of yours.'

The maid put her hand on my arm with a swift movement.

'Please don't get me wrong, Mr Faraday. I'm not trying to interfere. I just have Mrs Freeman's interests at heart. I know her attitude.'

'You seem to know a lot about me and my business,' I said.

The girl gave me a mischievous smile.

37

'I keep my eyes open, Mr Faraday.'

'How come you spotted me for a gumshoe?' I said.

Adele smiled again.

'The name rang a bell. I went out back into the kitchen quarters. I keep all the old *Examiners* there. They ran a picture of you over some case you cracked around five, six weeks ago.'

I looked at her admiringly. 'You ought to be on my staff,' I said. 'Not that I run to a staff.'

The girl raised her eyebrows.

'But if you had . . . ?'

I grinned.

'Something like that,' I told her. 'What did you mean just now?'

'About keeping me informed? Nothing out of line, Mr Faraday. It's just that I'm so fond of Mrs Freeman and this dreadful business has upset everyone.'

'Everyone?' I said.

The maid nodded.

'Just the staff here, beside Mrs Freeman. Myself, the gardener and the housekeeper. Mrs Irons is away on vacation at the moment and I'm looking after things.'

She hesitated and lowered her voice like we might be overheard in the vast open space of the hall.

'It's just that if there's anything really bad maybe you could tell me first. I'd like to cushion any further bad shocks. Mrs

Freeman's suffered enough.'

I stared at her for a long moment. She was a pretty good looker now that I came to give her a closer examination.

'You want to protect her, is that it? What further bad news could there be? Beyond murder, that is.'

Adele made a supple shrugging movement with her shoulders.

'The newspaper said . . .'

She broke off and bit her lip. I looked up toward the elegant circular window light at the head of the stairs where mellow sunshine made fretted patterns on the balustrades.

'You don't believe all that newspaper junk, surely. If Freeman was a homosexual and he and his wife were as close as you say someone would have found out years ago.'

The girl's face cleared. She nodded slowly, the darkness lifting from her eyes.

'I guess you're right, Mr Faraday. But I'd still be grateful if you would come to me first. You can trust me.'

I looked at the small oval face lifted up to mine.

'I'm sure I can, Adele,' I said. 'I'll keep you in touch.'

The girl put her hand on my arm.

'Thank you, Mr Faraday. I'd appreciate it.'

She led the way back at a fast clop like she was glad an awkward interview had terminated. I was still chewing a few things over in my mind when we got to the front door.

She stopped again then, moved closer to me.

'There's something else you should know, Mr Faraday. There's been another Red Dragon murder. The flash came through on the radio a while back.'

'Mrs Freeman told me,' I said.

There was no time to go on. A big maroon Caddy was just gliding to a halt in front of the entrance. The driving door slammed and then an elegant, affable-looking man with silver-grey hair was striding up to meet us.

2

The girl interpreted the query in my eyes correctly.

'That's Mr Leo van Dorn, Mrs Freeman's uncle,' she whispered while the silver-haired man was still out of earshot. 'He's the family's only surviving relative.'

I nodded, keeping my face blank, as I was standing in the full sunlight of the porch.

'Not a word to anyone about my being retained by Mrs Freeman,' I said out the corner of my mouth. 'The fewer who know the better.'

The girl smiled at the big man who was looking from the maid to me with polite curiosity on his massive, tanned features.

'This is Mr Faraday, a business friend of Mr Freeman,' the girl said quickly. 'He just came to express his condolences.'

'Very kind of you, I'm sure, Mr Faraday,' van Dorn said heavily, giving me a bone-crushing grip with his big right hand. 'A terrible business, sir.'

'Dreadful,' I said, giving him my Academy Award winning performance.

He threw me a shrewd glance. He had broad, open features and faded blue eyes beneath the greying hair. Combined with a perfect set of teeth they gave him the air of an ageing matinee idol. I thought I might have seen him somewhere but I couldn't place him for the moment.

With a mumbled apology he turned to the girl.

'How is Mrs Freeman today? I've brought her some flowers and a few other little things that might distract from some of her present troubles. Perhaps you could fetch them from the car later.'

The maid nodded, glancing from the big man to me as though in affirmation.

'That's very kind of you, sir.'

Van Dorn's faded blue eyes turned back cursorily to me.

'Not at all. I am her uncle, you know.'

His manner had changed now and he became brisker.

'What is your business, Mr Faraday?'

'You might call it people,' I said.

His eyes opened a little wider.

'Public relations?'

'Something like that,' I told him.

Adele had a secret little smile at the corners of her lips as she went down toward the red Caddy. She came back with the large floral display in an expensive cellophane box from a famous L.A. florist and with several other packages done up in gift paper.

'You mustn't spoil her, Mr van Dorn,' she said reprovingly.

The big man in the well-cut grey suit with the pale pink shirt and matching tie shook his head sadly.

'That's impossible at the present time,' he said.

He gave me another bone-crushing grip.

'Well, I mustn't keep you, Mr Faraday. Nice to have met another of Deirdre's friends. I'd better get along inside now.'

'See you again, perhaps,' I said.

'I certainly hope so.'

He disappeared into the house. The girl, after giving me a brief, hesitant smile, followed on behind in a vain effort to keep up.

I watched until the big main door had closed behind them. I had a lot to think about on my drive across town but the Freeman number's cheque made a comforting glow around my chest muscles as I drove.

CHAPTER SIX

1

Stella was just shutting up shop when I arrived back at the office. She was working late tonight. She smiled faintly as I gave her a rundown on my afternoon.

'You see, Mike. Attention to detail. And a dainty tea thrown in.'

I threw her a lop-sided grin. I'm pretty good at them and Stella fell for it. She sighed heavily.

'I suppose that means you want coffee on top of all the other stuff you've already had.'

'It wouldn't come amiss,' I said.

I locked the waiting-room door while she went back to the alcove to brew up. I went on over to my desk and stared at the material Stella had left on it. I scribbled my signature at the bottom of three letters in her impeccable typing, folded and sealed them. I didn't bother to read them. I'd been all through that before and there was never anything needing correction.

Stella came back and sat on the edge of my desk and stared at me.

'You have an assignment, Mike?'

I smiled.

'How did you guess?'

'You always wear a goofy expression when you can see your way through financially to the next month.'

I didn't bother to top that.

Deirdre Freeman isn't satisfied with official efforts over her husband,' I said. 'And she doesn't like the newspaper smears.'

Stella's blue eyes were fixed on mine. I went on a little more quickly than I had intended.

'She came up with plenty of the folding stuff,' I said.

I got out the cheque from my wallet and passed it to her. Stella's eyes were wide and round as she stared at the figures.

'I'll pay this in first thing in the morning,' she said.

'The manager will be pleased,' I told her.

Stella smiled faintly and went over to the large-scale map of L.A. behind which is the office safe. It can be opened with a sardine can key but it gives Faraday Investigations a sense of security.

She put the cheque away and went back to the alcove. She was silent until we were drinking the coffee. She sat in her usual place in the client's chair, her notebook at her elbow.

I gave her a brief rundown of the dialogue over at the Freeman number's place. Stella frowned as I went on.

'This Filipino girl seems to know a good deal about the set-up.'

'People like that always get close to their employers,' I said. 'Sometimes it's a good thing. Sometimes not so good.'

Stella put down her coffee cup with a little chinking noise in the oppressive silence of the office.

'You think it's a good thing in this case?'

'I don't know yet,' I said. 'I haven't known the girl long enough.'

Stella smoothed down one immaculate eyebrow with the tip of an elegant finger.

'Or the mistress,' she murmured.

I let that one alone as well. There were too many comebacks. Stella studied her notes.

'You think the Freeman girl's grief is genuine, Mike.'

'You're getting cynical,' I said.

Stella shrugged, tossing the gold bell of her hair.

'I'm just being practical. Freeman was a rich man. So now Deirdre Freeman gets everything.'

'We don't know that,' I said.

Stella made an elegant little snorting noise down in her throat.

'The wife always gets everything under California law,' she said. 'Even when the husband dies intestate.'

'Sounds pretty painful to me,' I said. 'But you have a point. And Freeman was inclined to throw money around like confetti when he was playing the ponies, according to the wife.'

Stella stared at me in silence for a moment.

'So there you are. What about the uncle, the van Dorn character?'

'Pleasant enough guy,' I said. 'Seemed very concerned about her. The maid said he was the only surviving relative.'

Stella looked thoughtful.

'Does anyone else up there besides Deirdre Freeman know you're a private investigator?'

'The maid,' I said. 'She recognised me from a piece in the *Examiner*. She seems safe enough. Though the fewer people who know I'm on the case for the moment the better. The police may have a good deal more information than they've given out to the press.'

'McGiver could help there,' Stella said. 'It's on his beat.'

'We'll see,' I said.

I took another sip at my coffee, watching the steam from the surface of my cup rising lazily to the ceiling. I remembered something then I should have mentioned before.

'The Freeman girl and the maid said something about another dragon killing.'

Stella nodded, a serious expression in her eyes.

'I went out for a while and picked up a late edition,' she said. 'There's a short piece on the front, obviously dropped in at the last minute. And another mention in stop press.'

I took the *Examiner* from her and noted

she'd already circled the article ready for scissoring.

The victim this time was a character called Albert Petty. He was a 42-year-old TV producer who'd been found naked and shot in the back of the head in his apartment. The details were pretty lurid and even in the *Examiner*'s toned-down prose I could imagine the set-up. The more sensational tabloids would have had a field day.

There was a fairly sharp shot of the victim printed alongside the four-paragraph story downpage. The name or the face didn't mean anything to me. He carried the tattoo mark in the same place as the others, the report said.

I finished off the main story in silence and turned to the stop press Stella had mentioned. That carried the usual bromide about the police expecting early results and that Detective Lieutenant McGiver of Homicide had also been assigned to the latest shooting.

Stella watched me finish my coffee in silence.

'Might be an idea to see McGiver while the case is still hot,' she said.

'Or the corpse still cold,' I said.

Stella made a little moue.

'You know what I mean, Mike,' she said softly.

'Don't push so hard,' I said. 'I'll take a look in at Police H.Q. on the way home.'

I pushed my cup toward her for a re-fill.

47

'I'm practically on my way,' I said.

2

McGiver's office was a four by two plywood cubicle on the third floor of Central Police H.Q. building and I gumshoed my way up through the litter of peanut shucks and match-stalks, avoiding the reception area with its gimlet-eyed sergeants and waiting press men.

The breeze had been freshening up the sidewalks as I'd driven across town earlier but the stale atmosphere in here was so strong it seemed to catch at the back of one's throat and made breathing difficult. I wondered why people like McGiver and Captain Dan Tucker stuck it; the City's budget must be close to breaking down. The whole of law and order was breaking down, come to that.

I gave up the third-rate philosophising and padded across the worn linoleum to the door which said Detectives. There was no-one around when I poked my head through but the steady pecking of ancient typewriters sounded from half-open doors farther up the corridor.

McGiver's had a card on it in a tarnished brass holder which made the set-up look even more impermanent, like he himself might be slung off the force at any moment. Though I guessed it meant nothing more than that the occupants of this rabbit hutch changed about from time to time.

There was no answer to my discreet tap so I went on in. McGiver sat behind his battered desk with its piles of bundled reports, his wary eyes fixed on the waste-basket. He didn't look up from batting crumpled balls of paper into the basket with the handle of an old paper-knife.

'Lucky to find you in.'

'No luck about it,' he said. 'Your secretary phoned to say you were coming over so I stayed on.'

He glanced at the police issue clock hanging on the wall.

'I should have been off duty half an hour ago.'

'With a Murder One investigation on your hands?' I said.

He grinned faintly.

'I just got back. I've had five hours sleep in the last four days. Time to hit the sack.'

'You're lucky,' I said. 'You might have been involved in a crime-wave.'

McGiver gave his teeth a brief airing.

'In which case I might just hand in my badge.'

I looked at the clock too, taking the rickety chair McGiver indicated.

'What time was that,' I said. 'When Stella rang?'

'About an hour ago,' he said.

I grinned.

'She was pretty sure of me. I hadn't even gotten back to the office by then.'

'You didn't come here for social chit-chat,' he said. 'What's the beef?'

'No beef,' I said. 'I'd just like a little information.'

McGiver's eyes were wary again now. 'What sort of information?'

I shrugged.

'The sort that might not get into the newspapers.'

McGiver straightened up at the desk as the phone buzzed. He picked it up and listened intently.

'Not my department,' he said crisply. 'Try extension 53.'

He put the phone back on its cradle. For the first time then I could see how tired he was.

'This character Petty was a well-known homo in TV and film circles,' he said. 'Seems like the girls must be falling out.'

'I didn't mean him,' I said. 'I've been retained by Freeman's wife. Information restricted to you, of course. She's not happy about the press reports.'

'Who is?' he said. 'I'm not responsible for the crap they print. These Red Dragon tattoos gave them a field day.'

'What's your own opinion?' I said.

McGiver half-closed his eyes and stared up at the ceiling.

'Badges of rank,' he said. 'The Dragons are a well-known homosexual outfit. They even have their own underground magazine. My guess is someone doesn't like them.'

'That seems fairly obvious,' I said mildly. 'What about weapons.'

McGiver stirred in his chair.

'Same calibre throughout. You read the papers. Different weapons, though.'

'Which means?' I said.

McGiver put out one hand and batted another paper ball into the basket. It made a clean arc and hit dead centre. Not bad reflexes for a man who'd been up all those hours.

'Anything or nothing, Mike. Could have been the same guy switching pistols. Or some sort of vigilante organisation which is not keen on AIDS spreading around the community.'

'Thanks for your help,' I said.

McGiver grinned.

'I could do with some myself,' he admitted. 'Freeman's wife is convinced he isn't a homosexual,' I said.

McGiver sighed.

'That's the sad part, Mike. No wife wants to believe her husband is involved in anything like that.'

He pushed over a sheaf of documents.

'You want to read the autopsy reports?'

I shook my head.

'Not unless they're sensational.'

McGiver frowned.

'There's nothing in them that struck me as out of the ordinary. That is, for my line of business. But then I'm used to corpses with their brains splattered over the walls and furniture. It's the commonplace of the trade, you might say.'

'But you would tell me if you come across anything interesting,' I said. 'Particularly about Jerry Freeman, of course.'

'Sure, Mike,' McGiver said absently. 'Especially if you let me know how you're doing.'

'When did I ever hold out,' I said.

McGiver sighed, taking his eye off the waste-basket.

'We won't go into that,' he said heavily.

'You checked on all the tattoo parlors, of course,' I said.

McGiver sat upright, shook his head and put his hands up to his eyes. He remained hunched over for a few seconds, like fatigue had overcome him.

'From here to San Francisco and back,' he said in a muffled voice. 'Those tattoos were done with a special ink and some unusual method. Part of the society initiation, I guess. But we're still working on it.'

I nodded.

'Thanks, anyway. Sorry to keep you from your rest.'

'That's all right, Mike,' McGiver said.

He took his hands away from his eyes, blinking like the light from the low-powered bulbs in here was disturbing them.

'Don't leave it too late with Stella,' he said

irrelevantly.

'I don't know what you mean,' I said.

McGiver gave a dry chuckle.

'Some guys don't know when they're well off,' he told the filing cabinet.

I gave him one of my long, intense looks, thanked him again and went on out, leaving him staring at the fly-specks on the walls.

It was dark outside now and I fumbled around with the key to the Buick's driving door in the big police car-park in rear. I was just opening it when a hand the size of an eight-pound hambone showed up alongside mine and slammed the door closed.

CHAPTER SEVEN

1

I didn't turn around or do anything clsc in a hurry. A character with a hand that size could re-arrange my spinal cord in one or two easy movements. And then play pin-ball with my skull for afters.

'Good evening,' I said.

There was a harsh grunt in the warm darkness at my elbow.

'You might call it that,' said a voice that sounded like dirty water running down a dark tunnel in one of L.A.'s less salubrious sewers.

If you know what I mean. I figured the guy might have a speech defect.

He might have a brain defect too so I didn't make any silly moves. Not that I was carrying the Smith-Wesson today. It wasn't that kind of case from my point of view. Yet.

Something about the size of a brontosaurus moved at the corner of my eyeline. It was like a mountain shifting in the darkness. A moment or two later a match flared, lighting up a face of hammered steel with wary eyes. The guy had shoulders that made Johnny Weissmuller look like the nine-stone weakling in the magazine ads.

For the rest all I could see was some sort of dark, double-breasted suit and a snap-brim fedora of the kind I thought had gone out with Bogart movies. Not that they've gone out; just the fashions depicted in them. I wondered where this guy got his props from. But I thought it impolite to ask. He reminded me of Laird Cregar in one of his seedier roles.

Except that he was Cregar three times larger than life. Assuming one could absorb the fact. I was having some difficulty. The match went out then. I guessed he had just been checking on me.

'You're Mr Faraday. The private cop.'

They were statements, not questions.

'I have been called other things,' I said. 'But that's broadly correct.'

I stepped back to get a better view of the

giant. That was my first mistake. The ham-bone came from nowhere in the cloying darkness and gently patted me back into orbit again. My arm felt like it was being wrenched out of its socket.

'Please stay close to me, Mr Faraday,' the glottal voice went on. 'I have a little proposition for you.'

'That's nice,' I said.

The huge man nodded ponderously. My eyes were more used to the darkness out here now and I could take in the detail. Each more unlikely than the last. He must have been over seven feet tall for starters. I decided that fact would do for the time being. I'd already felt the quality of his muscles. They were tensile steel.

'We hope so,' the big man said.

'You got a name?' I said, more to gain a little time than anything else.

Though this was a police car-park there was no law around. It figured.

'You can call me Big Harry,' the giant said.

'That's nice too,' I said.

'Enough talk for the moment, Mr Faraday,' Big Harry said. 'It's not private enough here.'

'I was just beginning to like it,' I said.

The man-mountain grunted. He opened my driving door.

'We take your heap.'

'You sure you won't be cramped?' I said. 'I should have brought my sun-roof model.'

The big man put his sheet-metal face down toward mine.

'I'll punch a hole in the roof if I want more air, mister,' he said without malice.

I got in quickly, waited for him to go around to the passenger door. I didn't try anything. A moment later I saw side-lights wink on in my rear mirror. Like I figured the big man had company. I could see the faint outlines of two men in the sedan behind now.

My business with McGiver and with the Freeman girl was obviously known. It could only be that. There was nothing else anyone would want me for. Unless they were writ-servers. Somehow, I didn't think so.

The right-hand side of the Buick lurched violently as Big Harry got in. I started the motor. He sat impassive. By the light of the dashboard instruments I could see my first impressions had been vague indications of the reality. This was a character who could tear a man limb from limb with his bare hands.

So he didn't need to make useless displays of force. He exuded strength and menace without exerting himself. Leastways, so far as I was concerned. So I decided to take it easy with the wisecracks.

'I'm having a busy day,' I said.

'Are you,' he said politely.

He kept his gaze dead ahead through the windshield as we rolled forward but I could sense that his huge body was tensed, ready to

56

move if I made any untoward gesture.

'Where to?' I said.

'Right,' he said. 'Just a short drive.'

I did like he said, noting the sudden yellow flare of head-lamps as the car behind turned to the right too, keeping about a hundred yards in rear as we idled down the boulevard.

The traffic had thinned out this time of the evening and I had time to notice small details, like a man tying his shoelace, momentarily outlined like a Lotte Reiniger shadow film against the windows of a boutique.

'You know Charley's Club,' the big man said after a moment.

I glanced at the windshield, saw the tail was still following.

'I can find it,' I said.

'I'll remind you if you make a false move,' Big Harry told me.

I accelerated up a little as we got away from traffic lights. The huge man's hand was on mine in a fraction.

'You almost forgot our friends,' he said gently.

I pulled in to the kerb and waited, the motor throbbing in the humid night until the lights changed again and the tail car caught up with us.

'Your friends are pretty law-abiding,' I said.

The big man chuckled. The liquid voice sounded like storm water roaring down the drains now.

'You'll like my friends, Mr Faraday,' he said. 'They're law-abiding all right. They wouldn't want any hassle with a traffic cop this time of the evening.'

So he had a sense of humour too. That was worth knowing. Though how I could turn it to advantage I couldn't figure.

I didn't think I was in any real physical danger for the moment. Not unless I crossed Big Harry. And I didn't intend to do that. I thought it more likely that someone wanted to talk to me. Maybe to find out what I knew. Or to warn me off the case.

I gave up beating my brains out then and concentrated on the driving.

2

Charley's Club was and is a big brick box on an off-boulevard location that had been at various times a brewery, a warehouse and a TV rental operation. Some years ago it was clumsily converted into one of the sleazier night-spots; a combination drinking-club, bar, dance-joint and cabaret, all operating at the lower end of the scale.

I didn't have any cause to revise my opinion this evening from what I saw of the set-up. A three or four-piece orchestra was pumping out some sort of blues number in the far distance as I drew the Buick up in the alley alongside the club, which was already cluttered with parked automobiles opposite big red notices which said; STRICTLY RESERVED.

It was around nine o'clock when we got there and I eased out the driving door, conscious that the big man's friends had drawn up the far end, blocking my exit. Not that I was inclined to duck out; not without the Buick. And I hadn't made my reputation in L.A. by being the ducking kind.

Something of the same sort might have crossed Big Harry's mind because he gave me a bleak smile as he opened the passenger door opposite. The Buick's bodywork seemed to go up all of six inches once it was relieved of his weight. No-one quit the automobile parked in the distance. But then it wasn't necessary. Big Harry would have needed a small army to subdue him if he'd turned nasty. And I had nothing but my fists and my knowledge of judo. Not that the latter would have helped me in this situation. I would have needed an iron bar to make much impression on those shoulders and that neck.

'You're sensible, Mr Faraday.'

I shrugged.

'I try to be. Will you lead or shall I?'

The straight mouth opened up half a millimetre.

'You're very funny, Mr Faraday. You lead, I think. I'll tell you where to go.'

He stood aside to let me pass and I walked up a short flight of cement steps to a fire door

59

which proclaimed its function in big red letters on a white rectangle. We were in a dingy passage where naked bulbs burned in fittings in the side walls. The floor was cement too and there was a smell of stale cooking and cheap perfume in the air.

The sound of the orchestra was louder now and above it I could hear the clink of glasses and the low, languid sound of equally stale conversation. I glanced at the big man. He had his gaze fixed down toward the dusty floor and his eyes were shadowed by the brim of the fedora.

He was so big his shoulders seemed to brush the walls as he walked. He ushered me on and we went up a short flight of concrete steps edged with a black metal handrail. There were a few cheap colour photographs on the walls of equally cheap-looking peroxide strippers who'd once honoured the establishment with their art, if the captions were to be believed.

There was no-one around and the place seemed half-deserted. The action, whatever it was, was obviously elsewhere. We passed several doors which had stars made of silver paper pasted clumsily on to the wooden panelling. I smelt the sour smell of defeat and blighted hopes in here.

I glanced back over my shoulder, aware of Harry's palm, feeling as big as an open umbrella, in the small of my back.

'Pretty nice lay-out, eh?' he said

unconvincingly.

'If you like that sort of thing,' I said.

Big Harry shrugged.

'I do, mister,' he said in that strange liquid voice. 'Some pretty classy dames have been through these dressing rooms.'

'You sound like you have a share in the place,' I said.

The big man shook his head. I could see the gesture out the corner of my eye as he was almost abreast of me again now.

'So it isn't Earl Carroll's,' he said defensively. 'So what? And they get some great bands here.'

'Who's arguing?' I said.

He gave a genuine grin then, showing strong, even white teeth.

'I'm an enthusiast for clubs,' he said. 'I come alive after dark.'

'You must be quite vivacious during the daytime too,' I said.

He looked at me suspiciously for a moment, then shook his head again.

'I don't know what that means. But you're not my problem. It's for Mr Rich to decide.'

'Whoever he might be,' I said.

The vast man shrugged.

'That his real name?' I said.

Harry gave a thin smile.

'What do you think?' he told the brown-painted brick walls we were still passing. We turned right now, down a bisecting corridor.

'It's just an accommodation,' I said. 'Mr

Rich hired a room for an hour, especially for this interview.'

Big Harry looked sharply behind him, like he thought we might be tailed.

'Keep talking, Mr Faraday. I'm paid to listen. I don't have to answer.'

'Indeed you don't,' I told him.

We stopped in front of the last of the doors in this section of corridor. This one had two stars on it. For a minute I thought we'd come to see Mae West.

Big Harry tapped deferentially and we waited in a heavy, cloying silence. It was hot in here and I could feel a small bead of sweat trickling down my right cheek.

Presently there was a muffled reply and the huge man opened up the door. He smiled at me reassuringly.

'Mr Faraday to see you, Mr Rich,' he said.

The vast palm was on my back again as I went on in.

CHAPTER EIGHT

1

Mr Rich, when I got to see him, was a small, balding man with a thin black smear of mustache and pebble glasses which made him look something like Tojo in one of the old war-time newsreels. He wasn't at all what I'd expected and I stared at him in surprise for a moment as he got up awkwardly from behind a shabby desk in the small, bare room.

I knew then my hunch about it being hired for the occasion was right. For one thing this man didn't belong here. He was ill at ease with his assignment, whatever it was, and his well-cut suit and carefully groomed exterior didn't sit at all with his seedy surroundings.

I put him down as a lawyer or maybe some company executive who'd been briefed for an interview he was badly equipped to conduct and had no stomach for.

He looked at me carefully from behind the pebble glasses and waved me nervously to a wooden chair in front of the desk.

'Do sit down, Mr Faraday. I must apologise for this method of bringing you here.'

'Think nothing of it,' I said. 'I get all sorts of unusual invitations in my racket. What's yours?'

The nervous eyes behind the glasses blinked.

'I don't quite follow . . .'

'Your racket,' I said. 'You must be in one or you wouldn't have had me brought here like this.'

That stung and I noted with satisfaction the red patches spreading on the cheekbones. To cover his inward agitation he made a great business of sitting behind the desk and fooling with some papers he had there.

Before he could recover I hit him again.

'The police would be interested in your presence here, Mr Rich. These Red Dragon murders . . .'

The bald man half-got up in the chair and gave a strangled squawk.

'Really, Mr Faraday! You're taking things entirely too much for granted.'

'I don't think so,' I said levelly. 'You've got enough muscle out there in the corridor to hold up a U.S. Marine Division. Plus two goons in the automobile at the mouth of the alley. You obviously represent the brain end. The only real thing I'm working on at the moment is the Red Dragon kills. So what's your angle?'

For a minute I thought the bald man was going to blow a gasket. He opened his mouth a few times like he was gasping for air. While he was still recovering himself I went on.

'You've no objection to me smoking?'

I reached for my inside pocket.

Rich gave me a frozen smile.

'By no means, sir. Please indulge yourself.'

I lit up while he went on pasting his nerves together. The scratch of the match against the box seemed to irritate him even further. I decided to keep up the pressure.

'You're out of your depth, Mr Rich,' I said. 'Your boss should have come himself.'

He sat hunched at the desk, staring at its

scratched surface, his hands tightly pressed together to stop their trembling. I knew then that all my suppositions about him were correct. A deathly white had overlaid the red patches on his cheeks. I'd made my point. There was no sense in keeping it up.

I feathered out blue smoke toward the ceiling, keeping my eyes on his face until he was forced to return my glance.

'I don't like the character out in the corridor,' I said. 'I'm sure you don't either. So we make sure not to upset him.'

A faint shudder passed through the bald man's frame.

'You are certainly correct there, Mr Faraday. A horrible creature. I'm sure I don't know why . . .'

He stopped suddenly, looked at his nails again.

'Why your client employs him,' I finished.

Rich put his lips together, contorting his face into a prim, old-maidish expression.

'We're drifting away from the point, Mr Faraday,' he reminded me. 'Without going into detail I'm empowered to make you a certain financial offer.'

'Things are looking up,' I said. 'What sort of financial offer?'

The bald man's head held a sudden glaze of sweat under the naked bulbs that were suspended from the ceiling.

'Would five thousand dollars interest you,

Mr Faraday?'

The atmosphere in the room seemed to have gotten close and thundery. I caught Rich's eyes on mine, pinned them as I leaned forward to stub out my cigarette on a corner of the desk.

'You're well-named,' I told him. 'Just who does this generous offer come from?'

Baldilocks shook his head. There was a wry expression on his face now. I pegged him for a lawyer then. I'd seen that same look too often in court-rooms to mistake it.

'That would be telling, Mr Faraday. The offer is a genuine one, I can assure you.'

'I've no doubt,' I said. 'Let's hear the rest of the proposition.'

The bald man looked startled.

'The proposition, Mr Faraday?'

'This is carrying caution too far,' I told him. 'The proposition. What am I supposed to do for it?'

Rich tapped the bundle of papers in front of him.

'It's what you're not to do which is the important aspect, Mr Faraday,' he said gently. 'That is where my client's interests lie.'

'I'm still listening,' I said. 'You mentioned five thousand.'

Rich had an envelope in his hand. He'd just taken it from the bundle of papers. It was a

66

thick brown manila; it was bulky and it crackled slightly as he turned it over and over in his thin, agitated hands. I didn't have to see the greed in his eyes to know what was in it.

'Cash, Mr Faraday.'

He licked fleshy lips.

'Tax free. And in small denomination, untraceable notes, of course.'

'You mean to say they've been laundered?' I said.

The sharp, wounded look was back in the eyes now.

'Why do you persist in misunderstanding me, Mr Faraday. I should have thought my mission was clear enough.'

I was enjoying myself now.

'Sure,' I said. 'You want to bribe me but you're still pussyfooting all around the subject. Suppose I tell you?'

Futile rage and annoyance swept across the bald man's face.

'Tell me what, Mr Faraday?'

'About what I'm not to do, Mr Rich. I have a client. She wants a murder turned over. She wants the killer found. Or the person behind the killer. You wouldn't be the person behind the person, would you?'

The bald man's face was a mask of perspiration. He gave a strangled snort and reached for his collar like it was choking him.

'You have the most extraordinary ideas, Mr Faraday,' he said unconvincingly.

'They're the only ideas that make sense,' I told him. 'And if I don't agree, our friend comes in.'

Rich shivered, a look of distaste on his face.

'Crudely put, Mr Faraday. And I'm sure neither of us want that.'

'We live in a crude world, Mr Rich,' I said. 'Let's have it straight.'

The bald man gulped and took hold of his ragged nerve-ends.

He stabbed convulsively with his forefinger at the envelope in front of him.

'Since you insist on me spelling everything out, Mr Faraday, this is the deal. Here is the five thousand dollars, as I've already indicated. All you have to do is to leave the Freeman case alone.'

He licked dry lips.

'Let dead men lie.'

'Your principal would love that,' I said. 'And if I don't?'

Rich turned down the corners of his mouth in a sour, bitter grimace.

He shrugged.

'Well, then, Mr Faraday, I cannot be held responsible for the consequences.'

I stared at him for a long second.

'I can imagine,' I said.

He turned the envelope over, his eyes wheedling.

'What do you say, Mr Faraday? Here's the money.'

'Keep it,' I said. 'I'll think about it.'

He nodded slowly, disappointment mingled with fear on his face.

'And that is your last word.'

'You must be going deaf as well,' I told him. 'I said I'll think about it. When do we next meet?'

He still had the sorrowful expression on his face.

'We'll contact you, Mr Faraday. I do urge you most earnestly to come to terms with this situation.'

I got up quickly.

'I'll turn it over in my mind, Mr Rich. I can't say fairer. Question is, do I leave here peaceably or not?'

A look of swift astonishment passed over the bald man's face.

'Of course, Mr Faraday. There is simply no question of that.'

'You'd better let Kong know,' I said. 'Otherwise he might dismember me for dropping cigarette ash on his toecap.'

Rich nodded frostily, putting the envelope full of money back in his pocket.

'I will have a word with him. If you will step in there, Mr Faraday.'

I went over to the far door he indicated. The place was a small washroom with barred windows. I sat down on the toilet seat and listened to the mumbled colloquy coming from behind the door. After about five minutes

69

there was a nervous tap and it opened. Rich was framed in the lintel.

'You have three days, Mr Faraday. I will see you again then. I will name the time and place.'

'My pleasure,' I said.

I went on out and left him standing there. I walked back through the dusty, echoing brick corridors where nothing stirred, listening to the modern jazz pumping faintly in the distance. There was no sign of Big Harry. Not that I'd have expected there to be.

Like I figured too there was no sedan blocking the entrances to the alley. That still didn't stop me haunting my rear mirror all the way across town. When I got back to my rented house over on Park West I locked and bolted the doors and closed the drapes on all the ground floor windows.

Not that that would have stopped Big Harry. But it made me feel a little more secure. Then, before ringing Stella, I went up to the locked cupboard in my bedroom where I keep a small armoury of weapons and broke out of my favourite Smith-Wesson .38. It was that kind of case now.

CHAPTER NINE

1

'You can relax, Manny,' I said. 'Your fifty thousand is safe.'

Manny Richter blinked at me through the thin haze of cigar smoke that encircled his head. It was ten a.m. now and I'd dropped in at The Blue Moon on my way in to the office. The bulk of the Smith-Wesson made a reassuring pressure against my chest muscles as I shifted on the chair in front of his desk.

Richter's eyes widened in astonishment.

'That's great, Mike. How did you manage it?'

I grinned.

'Well, I didn't slap her around, that was for sure. I just asked. Apparently she has every intention of settling all Jerry Freeman's gambling debts. Unless I miss my guess your cheque will be through the mail before the week is out.'

Manny Richter raised his eyebrows. He sat down at his desk, pulled over a leather-bound book and started scribbling something on a sheet of mauve paper. Presently he finished with a grunt and tossed it over to me.

'For services rendered, Mike.'

I caught the cheque in mid-air and felt like

whistling when I read the amount. Seemed like I was at the top end of the private eye business for once.

'You haven't got your money yet,' I reminded him.

He gave his teeth another airing.

'Your word's good enough for me, Mike.'

'Well, I can always tear it up if she welshes on the promise,' I said. 'But she won't.'

The club owner looked at me shrewdly.

'Impress you, did she?'

I nodded.

'Absolutely square. They must have been a good deal in love.'

Manny looked at me gloomily. His cigar had gone out again.

'Tough,' he told the ceiling. 'Could you stand a drink?'

'Not this early in the morning,' I said. 'But there is something you can do for me.'

Manny spread his hands wide on his blotter with a theatrical gesture.

'Anything,' he said.

'Save the Academy Award stuff,' I said. 'It's just a little information. Some characters tried to bounce me off the case last night.'

Richter looked worried and shifted uneasily in his chair.

'My case?' he said.

'Give your nerves a rest,' I said. 'I wasn't talking about you. I was talking about the case I'm on. The Freeman number hired me to find out who killed Jerry. Someone else already knew about it. They sent a big thug to freeze me off. He did a great job too. Then they offered a wad of money to sweeten me up.'

Manny had control of himself now.

'It's a wonder your constitution can stand all these changes, Mike.'

'I make the jokes around here,' I told him. 'The character I'm talking about has a sheet-metal face, is over seven feet tall and goes under the name of Big Harry.'

'Sounds delightful,' Manny said. 'It doesn't ring a bell but I'll have some inquiries made.'

'I'd appreciate it,' I said. 'Discreetly, of course. Ring my office if you come up with anything.'

Manny nodded. He looked at me shrewdly.

'Seems pretty strange, doesn't it? You being tagged like that. Where's the leak coming from?'

I shrugged.

'It isn't very difficult to get a line on people in my racket. Once you start nosing around characters crawl out the woodwork. I went to see the wife of one of the murder victims. You can't keep that secret. Then I visit Police H.Q.'

Manny gave me one of his gloomy looks.

'I see what you mean. Plenty of leaks at Police H.Q. Someone could have reached for a phone while you were in with your friend.'

I grinned.

'Someone here could have done the same

when I first came to you.'

Manny looked aggrieved.

'Come on, Mike, you can't prove that.'

'I can't prove anything,' I told him. 'You didn't keep your debt beefs secret, did you?'

Manny changed gear on the dead cigar that stuck out of his brown, seamed face like it was a permanent fixture.

'That's true,' he admitted.

He gave me a frank stare.

'I wanted to go to sea when I was a boy.'

He shook his head.

'Thank Christ I resisted the temptation. I don't have a tattoo on me.'

His rare, dry laugh followed me all the way to the door.

2

Stella's eyes were very blue and very serious as she stared at me across the desk. The plastic-bladed fan kept on pecking at the edges of the silence, redistributing the warm, tired air. The bulk of the Smith-Wesson made a comforting pressure against my shoulder muscles as I shifted my weight in the swivel chair.

'So you had professional strong-arm men and an amateur Mr Big,' Stella said. 'Sounds interesting.'

'Sure,' I said.

'And should suggest one or two things,' Stella went on.

She got up without prompting and went over to the glassed-in alcove, walking with the firm, purposeful steps of a girl who had something on her mind. About the case I mean. Today she wore a pale blue silk dress with a plain leather belt at the waist and shoes to match the belt and I admired her action all the way.

But it was really too hot for that sort of thing and I got my beat-up brain back on Deirdre Freeman's assignment. I wondered how close she and the girl Adele were. The Filipino maid figured she knew all the family secrets; that could be useful.

But in my experience there were always areas which women like Mrs Freeman kept private, even from their most trusted servants. And there was no doubt people in her situation; lonely probably, with their husbands away a lot; became very dependent on those who worked for them.

Not that I didn't think she was speaking the truth for one moment. But it was unlikely that she would have unburdened herself of all her inmost thoughts to a stranger. Especially when she was being so defensive about the homosexual implications of the case.

I believed her on that point, not that it made any difference. I stared at the picture and other material that Stella had clipped from the *Examiner* for our files.

There were some obvious pointers when

looking for visual evidence of homosexuality. I couldn't see any in Jerry Freeman's frank, open features; that didn't prove anything, of course. Even some of the most aggressively male husbands had proved bi-sexual before now.

I put the cuttings back on top of the cardboard folder Stella had already numbered and filed. There wasn't much to go on and McGiver seemed like he was describing circles though he wouldn't admit that to someone like me. Stella was back now, arms folded across firm breasts, looking down at me with her disconcertingly frank stare.

'Such as what?' I said, taking up our conversation where it had broken off.

Stella wasn't fazed. But then she never is. She sat down delicately on the nearest corner of my desk and frowned at the toecap of one dazzlingly polished shoe.

'Mrs Freeman wants the murderer of her husband found. One of a series of homosexual murders. Each of the victims distinguished by a red dragon tattoo.'

'I follow you so far,' I said innocently.

Stella shot me a swift, hard look.

'Satire doesn't become you, Mike,' she said softly. 'You want to hear my ideas or not?'

'Certainly,' I said quickly.

Stella got up suddenly and went back to the alcove. She'd heard some slight difference in the sounds the percolator was making. I didn't

76

know how she did it but she was never wrong. She came back in a few moments and put my cup down on the blotter, went around the desk to the client's chair with her own. I stirred, watching the dusty sunlight at the window and the shimmer of the stalled traffic on the smog-filled boulevard outside.

Stella was back by the desk again, carrying a file and her handbag; she had the biscuit tin under her right arm.

'No need to help,' she said. 'I can manage.'

I grinned up at her.

'That's what I thought.'

I took the file from her before she could throw it, eased the tin out from under her arm. She was slightly flushed by the time I finished. She went around the desk and sat down in the client's chair, stirring her coffee with urgent little movements.

I nuzzled into my first with the usual sense of expectation. The first is always the best. I wasn't disappointed.

'You were talking about the Freeman kill,' I said.

Stella nodded, the gold bell of her hair glistening beneath the overhead lamp.

'Mrs Freeman didn't know her husband had the tattoo,' she said. 'That could bear looking into. The composition of the tattoos. A special ink, McGiver said. That should narrow it down.'

'The police didn't get anywhere,' I

reminded her.

Stella shrugged.

'So what? The police have to work through official channels. You have no such inhibitions.'

I stared at her through the steam rising from my cup. She had a point there. Like usual.

'And there's another thing, Mike. Maybe somebody respectable hired pros to take these people out, instead of doing it himself. It's been done before.'

'We have no motive yet,' I said.

Stella made an elegant little noise back in her throat.

'Blackmail, goof. There's lots of angles. One hardly needs motives with that sort of sub-world. Emotional jealousy; threat of exposure to one's colleagues in the business field.'

I kept my eyes fixed on Stella's face as she went on talking. It was a nice face to look at. And, like always, she was talking sense. Cogs were beginning to turn in my brain now.

'You might have something, honey,' I said. 'That last suggestion. That's just what Rich reminded me of. Some mild accountant or company lawyer. Forced by someone higher up to front for Big Harry and the muscle men.'

'There you are, then,' Stella said.

'Still lots of loose ends, too many possibilities,' I said.

Stella stared at me incredulously.

'That's what they pay you to find out,' she

said.

'That reminds me,' I told her.

I got out Manny Richter's cheque and passed it over. Her eyes opened wide.

'It's still months to Christmas,' she said.

I grinned.

'Pay it in with the other.'

'I've already been to the bank once this morning,' Stella said.

'Now you'll have to go again,' I told her.

She was already on the way to the alcove for the second cup.

'I'll get all this stuff typed up for you,' she said when she came back. 'Something may emerge when we set it all out properly.'

She was talking about the notes she'd been taking almost from the moment when I'd hit the office. She sat back in the client's chair and looked at me in silence for a moment.

'You know what you ought to be doing, Mikc,' she said at last.

I nodded.

'Rooting out the fancy artist who does the dragon tattoos which use the special ink,' I said.

Stella shot me a gleam of approval.

'Right,' she said decisively.

'Except that the police have failed,' I reminded her. 'And if these people belonged to some secret sort of homosexual organisation they might get the tattooing done in Seattle.'

'On the other hand,' Stella said in an

ominously quiet voice. 'It could be done right here in L.A.'

I drained my cup.

'Meaning what?'

Stella tapped with her gold pencil on very white teeth.

'Supposing it was a private person. An expert tattooist who'd maybe retired. Or who carries on business from an ordinary house or apartment. Or who's just moved into L.A. fairly recently.'

I got up from my chair.

'I won't argue about it.'

Stella smiled.

'Where will you be?' she asked.

'Around,' I said. 'I know a little man who's been useful on more than one occasion. He has his feet in many different worlds.'

'That must be awkward for him,' Stella said.

I shrugged.

'There's a pool hall where he usually hangs out. It's called Fat Fred's. I'll start there.'

'If I feel in need of a few frames I'll look over,' Stella promised me.

I went on out before she could think up anything else.

CHAPTER TEN

1

It was nearly lunch-time when I got to the section I wanted and I stopped in a diner for a bite to eat. I kept my eyes on the rear-mirror all the way across town but I couldn't see anything or anyone suspicious. That didn't prove a thing, of course. The nervous Mr Rich had said I'd got three days.

That was an unmistakable indication that Big Harry would be dropping on me from a great height after that. Which was mainly why I was carrying the Smith-Wesson. And a man like Big Harry cast an equally big shadow, both literally and metaphorically. So I was on my guard in case he and his colleagues didn't wait until the three days were up.

I had a lager with my lunch and I was suffering slightly from gas pains when I quit the diner. It always happens when I'm in a hurry. Christ, you're only thirty-three, Mike, I told myself; your stomach lining won't last out until you're fifty at this rate. I thrust the thought to the back of what was left of my mind and fought my way across a busy junction to the opposite sidewalk where Fat Fred's stood, squat and ugly, on a corner of the block. There was an old-fashioned wood staircase up the side to the third floor where the pool halls were and I clattered on up, uneasily conscious that I was too conspicuous here. The sun was burning through the haze now and I was in a lather of sweat by the time I got to the broad landing at the top. It was like dark velvet in the foyer beyond when I eased through the heavy glass-fronted doors and I stopped a moment to let my eyes adjust.

Then I went on into the first of the series of seven interconnecting halls where skeletal-looking figures shot pool under the green-shaded lamps. It was airless, hot and claustophobic in here and I went on quickly down the dim, shadowy interiors, looking for my man.

No-one took any notice; there was nothing but the reek of stale cigarette-smoke catching at the throat; the click of ivory connecting; and the occasional grunted monosyllable from the players. Some people spent their lives this this, for small two or three-dollar stakes. It wasn't my scene at all.

I was in the fourth hall now and I still hadn't found my man. I was beginning to think I'd run out of luck when I spotted a tall, bearded figure I knew. He was a long-time haunter of the dark and I'd managed to do him a favour or two when he was in a jam with the police one time a few years back.

He paused opposite me, making an elaborate scenario of a simple pot in the near corner of the table. 'Looking for someone in particular, Mr Faraday?'

'Just a social visit, Rocky. I wanted a word with Feeny Edwards.'

The bearded man shrugged, squinting down his cue like he figured it was curved or something.

'He was around here half an hour ago, waiting for a table,' he said. 'I think he went down the far end.'

I thanked him and moved on. I went through all the remaining rooms with a mounting sense of disappointment. I was in the sixth now. It was pretty crowded and there was so much smoke it was difficult to see the tables, let alone the players.

'I heard you was asking after me, Mr Faraday.'

The small, wizened man had materialized at my elbow. I blinked through the smoke.

'You heard good, Feeny.'

The beady eyes were free of guile.

'That's not all I heard, Mr Faraday.'

'We can't talk here,' I said.

Feeny drew me over to a darker area of the room, where worn leather benches were scattered about. He produced a bunch of keys on a ring from the pocket of his jacket.

'I keep the place clean and do odd jobs for the owner. He lets me have the use of a cubbyhole here.'

He unlocked a door and we went up a small

flight of stairs to a sort of loft which had a heavy beamed ceiling. But it was comfortable enough in a primitive fashion, with a table, several chairs; an electric stove for brewing up coffee; and a lot of colour pictures of a mildly scatalogical nature that were pinned on the unpainted timber walls.

'Pretty nice,' I said, looking at the unmade bed in the corner.

Feeny grinned crookedly.

'You might well say so, Mr Faraday. I slept in a lot worse.'

'What have you heard?' I said.

I sat down on one of the old slat-back chairs and offered him my pack. He looked like he could use them so I gave him the three-quarter full package. He opened a drawer in the table carefully and stashed it away. With his lined face, thin smear of white mustache beneath the reddened nose and the dusty thatch of hair on top of his bony skull he looked like one of those old thirties Life photographs of the dust bowl victims. But I didn't waste much time on the analogy.

'There's a guy called Big Harry doesn't like you,' he said.

I raised my eyebrows.

'Word gets around quickly.'

Feeny sat down deliberately at the table, sidewise on to me and squinted at the naked bulb hanging from the ceiling. Faintly, in the far distance, the games at the pool tables

84

below went on.

'In some instances, Mr Faraday.'

'Who is Big Harry?' I said.

Feeny hesitated.

'It could mean some money in your pocket,' I said.

The little man gave me another lop-sided grin.

'It could also mean a broken head. He could do it with his little finger in my case.'

'Who's going to know we've had this talk?' I said.

Feeny scratched around in his dusty hair for a moment.

'The big man's an out of town operator,' he said. 'That's all I know. But he's mean and hard. Doesn't carry a gun. Doesn't need one. He's been to L.A. two—three times to my knowledge. Each time there was trouble.'

'You know who he works for?' I said.

Feeny shook his head.

'Some big-shot in the East. Chicago, most likely. It's like baseball. He loans him out occasionally.'

I stared at him for a long moment, the cogs in my mind turning but getting nowhere.

'So your Mr Big in Chicago wouldn't necessarily be directly concerned with what was going on in L.A.'

Feeny shook his head.

'He's always missing when there's connections to be made, Mr Faraday. If you're tangling with

Big Harry—and my advice is, don't—it's a waste of time looking at Chicago. He'll have been hired by someone in L.A.'

'That's what I figured,' I said. 'But I'm grateful anyway.'

Feany's beady eyes narrowed.

'How grateful, Mr Faraday?'

I gave my teeth another airing.

'We'll see at the end of this interview, Feeny. What do you know about the Red Dragons?'

There was a faint tremor in the little man's finger-tips now.

'They're a sort of club, Mr Faraday. There are a lot of them around in the L.A. basin. Everywhere, for that matter. They go in for fancy initiation marks so they can identify one another.'

'There's no need to be coy,' I said. 'I know all that. I want some information about this particular group.'

'It's a club for queers,' Feeny said defiantly.

There was such disapproval in his tones I would have been amused any other time.

'I rather gathered that,' I said. 'It's the tattoo marks I'm interested in. It's done with special inks, I understand. The police have been unable to trace the tattooist. I thought you might be able to help me. They drew blank at the ordinary tattoo parlors. I figured it might be a man who's new to the area or retired maybe.'

Feeny fingered his chin with slow deliberation.

'You figured right, Mr Faraday. I might be able to help. For a consideration, of course.'

2

'Of course,' I said.

There was a long silence between us. It was hot up here among the beams and airless and I wondered how the little man stuck the conditions, especially after a night spent like that. But he seemed oblivious to the atmosphere, his small, beady eyes fixed brightly on my face.

'There ain't gonna be any trouble is there?' he said at last. 'I mean, for this guy.'

I shook my head.

'I shouldn't think so. I just want to ask him something about the tattoos, that's all.'

Feeny nodded solemnly.

'It's just a hunch, Mr Faraday. There was a guy around some while back. He's pretty old now and long retired. He flickered into my mind when I read the newspaper reports. He'd reintroduced some old techniques. From the East, I think. He used to practice privately from his house, after his partner died and he gave up his shop.'

I kept my eyes on his face.

'I'm listening,' I said.

'The information didn't come from me,'

87

Feeny said.

I sighed.

'I thought I already made it clear this was going to be discreet stuff.'

The little man blinked lazily.

'I just wanted to make sure we're on the same tram-lines, Mr Faraday,' he said ingratiatingly.

He leaned toward me and lowered his voice.

'Of course, it may be a bum steer. In that case you won't want your money back?'

I shook my head.

'I don't operate like that, Feeny. I thought you knew.'

The little man swallowed once or twice, his eyes far away now, focused somewhere up among the shadowy beams over our heads.

'The guy I have in mind must be pushing seventy by now. But he was still doing a few private jobs the last time I heard. It was these unusual colours I remembered. Like old paintings. I had a friend once, who had a cockerel tattooed on his back. Marvellous reds they were, like the thing was alive. When he flexed his back muscles I thought the damn thing was going to take off.'

'You can spare me the details, Feeny,' I said.

The little man looked aggrieved.

'You got no soul, Mr Faraday,' he complained. 'This guy is a real artist.'

'Has he got a name?' I said.

Feeny drew himself up at the table.

'I ain't seen a smell of your money, Mr Faraday,' he said.

'You're mixing your metaphors,' I said. 'But I get the point. I'll make it worth your while.'

Feeny raised his eyes to the ceiling again.

'That's more like it,' he said. 'This guy's called Lou Harper. I can tell you where he used to live. 1122 Romero Drive. That was maybe a couple of years back. That's all I know. Honest.'

'It's enough,' I said.

I believed him. I rummaged around in my wallet. Feeny sat there, his eyes big and round. I counted out a hundred bucks and pressed them into his suddenly sweating palm.

'It's too much, Mr Faraday,' he said through trembling lips.

'I could go on a three-week jag with this and do my health a lot of no-good.'

I grinned.

'Stick it in the bank, Feeny,' I advised him. 'There are hard times coming. I got a good expense account for this case. It doesn't come out of my pocket.'

Feeny brightened, sticking the bills in his table drawer and turning the key.

'Maybe I should have asked for more,' he told the ceiling beams.

I shook my head.

'You didn't ask for anything. But if you had asked for more you wouldn't have gotten it.'

I got up to go.

'You've been a real help,' I told him. And meant it.

'Be careful,' Feeny said. 'And you've never been here.'

'You're stealing my lines,' I said.

He gave me another lop-sided smile. He showed no inclination to move so I started picking my way toward the door through which we'd come in. It was in a corner under the eaves so that I had to stoop to unlatch it and get down the stair.

Feeny stopped me when I had the door half-open.

'Be careful, Mr Faraday,' he repeated. 'I'll sure as hell be that,' I said.

He shook his head.

'You don't get my drift. It's not just Big Harry.'

I turned, aware of the dusty wooden stair winding its way back down to the pool hall. I wondered how many hundred nights he'd stumbled up here with a skinful.

'Word gets around,' he said in a low voice, like he was talking to himself. 'Big Harry's bad enough. But he's got two others pros with him. They carry heavy iron.'

He sighed again.

'And they're ex-Marine trained. To use every kind of weapon. In every kind of situation.'

I stood there in the cloying silence for a moment longer but he didn't speak again.

'Thanks anyway,' I said in the end. 'I'll bear it in mind.'

He nodded gloomily and I went back down, locking the door behind me with the patent lock and picked my way out past the green-shaded lights and the ritual figures at the tables. I didn't see anyone or anything out of the ordinary but I unobtrusively transferred the Smith-Wesson to my trouser pocket where the butt felt cool and reassuring against my hand.

Even the smog and gasoline fumes smelt fresher in the street.

CHAPTER ELEVEN

1

Eleven-twenty-two Romero Drive was on a canyon location in an area that had once seen better days. That would have been in the twenties, of course, when Tom Mix probably lived there.

Right now the big frame houses with stone foundations and patios quarried from the surrounding hills were sagging visibly from decades-long exposure to sun, rain and salt air and most of them had peeling paint and a general air of neglect.

It was about an hour's drive where I was

going and it was late afternoon when I got there, the shadows stencilled long and heavy on the dusty ground. I pulled the Buick up in the shade of a flowering hedge and killed the motor. I'd left the Smith-Wesson on the passenger seat, covered by a magazine, and now I fished it out and put it back in my pocket just in case. I'd got Red Dragons on the brain by now but Big Harry and the two hit-men Feeny had mentioned had got me nervous.

To say nothing of the five tattoo killings so far. Or was it six. I was beginning to lose count. So far as I knew Big Harry had nothing to do with them. Contract men from out of town didn't hang around once they'd hit but lit out by plane for the East or wherever they'd come from.

I wasn't flattering myself they'd been brought in specially by someone to lean on me though the thought was a boost to my ego. Besides, it had been too quick.

I got out the driving door and closed it quietly behind me. The houses were well-spaced here with generous front lots to the houses, most of them sheltered by formal hedges or barriers of flowering shrubs.

I walked on down to get the lay-out. I almost passed the house I wanted because it had a drive that curved round from a narrow entrance without gates or other identifying features. I went on for a couple hundred yards more and gave the onceover to a few other properties.

There were no automobiles parked along the sidewalk and nothing suspicious that I could see. The sun was still hot on my cheek when I got to the end of my circuit and I retraced my steps on the other side of the boulevard, in the shade this time.

There was no-one around in the grounds of the houses except for a white-haired old lady up at the far end, who was struggling with a motor-mower that had given up the inclination to start and who was swearing at it vehemently between clenched teeth.

Normally I'd have gone over to give her a hand but this wasn't the afternoon and I left her to it. I went back and locked the Buick's driving door, checked the rest. Finally, I examined the mailbox that was located on an oak post about twenty feet down the drive. That had the faded stencil HARPER on the metal lid so Edwards' information had been right. Not that I'd expected him to welsh on me; I'd used him before and had always found his information accurate.

I went on up the drive, my feet gritting on the gravel, the sun glinting on the foliage, a slight dust rising and re-settling as my size nines disturbed the pebbles. There was no sound except that of the birds and, now and again, the more raucous noise of gulls.

Harper's place was on one of the highest

points in this location, at the edge of a bluff and now and again, through the fringing trees, I could see the faint glitter of the ocean. The Pacific was quiet today and the rusty red of the kelp beds, farther out, hardly undulated in the swell.

I was up near Harper's big clapboard house now. Its paintwork, gloss white except for some black on exposed beams was pretty good for this area but the grass of the lawn was long and badly neglected, the scorched yellow showing that it seldom benefited from a hose.

I might have thought the place was empty except that there was a dusty-looking VW parked in front of open garage doors to the right of the house.

My footsteps in the gravel echoed back from the facade of the big, three-storey structure. I went up the zig-zag flight of steps in front to the screen door and hit the bell-push. I could hear it echoing way back in its interior and then the building lapsed back into its silence.

A bluebottle or some other insect buzzed angrily in the heat and sweat was trickling in slow rivulets down the side of my face. I waited for perhaps a minute. Nothing stirred except for a slight wind in the tree-tops round about.

I hit the bell again, a nerve fretting in my cheek. There was still no response. I tried the inner door. It was locked like I figured. I went back down the steps and followed a path that led around and in rear of the house. Harper might be in the patio or working in his garden. He must be about somewhere if the VW meant anything.

The house was miles from anywhere and he would need transport to get back into town. Unless he was visiting with a neighbour. It hardly mattered to me. I'd got plenty of time this afternoon. I'd turned the end of the house now. There was another lawn in rear. The garden was quite small and apart from a deserted summerhouse there was nowhere else the owner could be.

The lot ended in a flowering hedge with a wire fence beyond and then the hillside fell to a shoulder of rock where a bluey-green fold of the Pacific showed. I didn't hang around here. The French windows giving on to the paved stone terrace gaped blackly. I hesitated a few seconds and then went on in.

2

It was cool and dim inside after the heat and glare and I paused to let my eyes adjust. The place was a living room, untidy, littered with read newspapers and magazines and cluttered with what looked like artist's materials. There were glazed jars and tins filled with brushes; one or two good water colours on the walls; a faint smell of turpentine and paints.

I felt a slight quickening of my pulse rate. I went down the room slowly, noting the way the light filtering in through the Japanese paper blinds undulated and swayed with the breeze that was coming in. I eased out the Smith-Wesson from the shoulder-holster and put it in my trouser pocket where I could get at it in a hurry.

I don't know why I did that. Just instinct I guess. Maybe strengthened by the memory of Big Harry and my three-day deadline from Mr Rich. I stood and looked at one of the water colours. This was a portrait of a rather effeminate-looking young man, stripped to the waist and obviously very proud of his physique. I stooped to read the initials and date at the right-hand bottom corner of the picture. It had been done by Harper all right.

So he was an artist as well as a tattooist. Like I said, Feeny Edwards' information was good. Deirdre Freeman's hundred dollars had been well spent. There was something else that tied in with the case and Edwards' information as well. There was a faintly disturbing homosexual quality about the picture; a narcissistic attitude both of the pose and glance on the part of the sitter.

My hunches were strengthening by the minute. If Harper was the man who had tattooed Mrs Freeman's husband then he'd known a great deal about the Red Dragon Society my informant had mentioned. Which might lead me to Freeman's murderer. If Harper was home I'd get the facts even if I had to beat it out of him.

Then I remembered he was an old man. An old man and perhaps a frightened man? Big Harry frightened me too and I was young and fit and used to dealing with the rough end of the P.I. business. So Harper would probably talk without too much trouble. Providing I found him.

What I wanted now was some evidence of the tattooist's art. I wouldn't find it here. It wouldn't be on public display where the casual visitor might see it. Especially if members of a homosexual society were paying Harper for these special designs. I tried to recall what Stella had typed from the sum of the knowledge gleaned from newspaper reports; McGiver's comments; and from what Edwards had told me.

I should have asked McGiver for a glimpse of the colour pictures of the autopsy. That would have given me the exact shade of the dragon tattoos. But I figured I'd know the shade if it was as special as people said it was. If Harper had an apartment here he used for tattooing private clients is would probably be upstairs and locked.

I went through the ground floor quickly. There was no-one around. I was feeling a faint fret of doubt now. The VW and the open window proved there had to be someone home. There had been no reply to my ringing and I'd heard no-one stirring. But I had a growing conviction that the house was occupied.

Maybe the old man was upstairs in bed sick? It was a possibility I hadn't thought of. Though there might be a more sinister explanation. I got out the Smith Wesson and fanned it in front of me as I mounted the creaking stairs. There was no way of avoiding the loose treads and I took off into orbit every time I hit one.

If there was anyone up there he couldn't fail to hear me coming. I could have been heard on the sidewalk outside. So my nerves were in a pretty ragged state by the time I got to the landing, lit by a dusty skylight. The stairs made a turn here and went up to the third storey. If Harper had a workroom it was probably up there. But I made sure first.

I went through the three bedrooms and bathroom on this floor. They were all empty and in the cases of the master bedroom and the bathroom the windows were wide open to let the air through. I didn't waste any more time. I went up the last flight of steps at a run.

There was just a wide landing here and two doors facing me. The first I opened revealed a room got up as a studio, with wood panelling and a big skylight giving a north light. I didn't waste time with the canvases stacked around. This place was obviously used for painting only.

I hesitated with my hand on the knob of the last door. If I failed here that left only the garage and my vaguely formed theories and Feeny Edwards' suppositions crumbled to nothing. I opened the door quickly, letting out a rush of hot air, the Smith-Wesson held high and wide.

I left the door open to clear the atmosphere. There was a strange odour here, mingling with the smell of paints and chemicals from the studio next door. There were green blinds drawn over the fanlights and I went across and let one up with a rushing whirr of rollers that seemed to set the echoes stirring for far longer than was natural.

The place was got up like a dental surgery with a wash-basin; large padded chairs with neck-rests; and drills and other instruments suspended from electric cables that came down from a point in the middle of the ceiling. There were colour pictures around the walls; some of the clients, others of different types of tattoo.

The far wall was covered with glass jars that contained chemical dyes or whatever it is that tattooists use for their craft. I went on over and glanced down the shelves. I soon saw what Edwards had meant. There were some very unusual shades here, some of them with unpronounceable Chinese names.

I opened up another of the blinds. Below the fanlight on this side was a small shelf with glass doors. There were two jars in particular which contained liquid of a startling red colour which seemed to glint and shine in the sunlight spilling in.

I used my handkerchief and eased back the glass partition, ignoring the greens and blues and golds of the other jar contents. I picked out the nearest containing the red pigment and held it up to the light. It was so shiny and brilliant it seemed to have life within it.

I've noticed that with some jewellery. This was certainly no ordinary dye and I was convinced I'd hit the jackpot. I couldn't make out the provenance of the stuff from the printed label. These were like the old-fashioned ones chemists used to use for glass containers in their shops. There are still a few around.

I unscrewed the lid of the jar and sniffed at the contents. It was extremely pungent and smelt of cloves and camphor mingled with a number of other subtle odours. I re-sealed it tightly and put it in my pocket. I could get McGiver's lab people to do an analysis and compare it with the red dragon tattoos on the victim.

I moved over to a bench whose work-top held a jumble of drawings. They were designs for various tattoos and I went through them quickly, putting the Smith-Wesson down on a corner of the bench. There was nothing of interest and I crossed to a big, nineteenth century armoire that was up against the opposite wall.

My foot kicked against something then; something which rustled and stirred. I bent down and picked it up. It was a piece of glossy art paper of the sort on which Harper had inscribed his designs. It was only a fragment, torn from something larger.

But it suddenly set my pulses racing. The design was in the same vivid colour as the dye in my pocket; and the scrap showed what looked like the corner of a wing. The red dragon . . .

I was still standing there when there came a high creaking noise which tore my nerves to ribbons and the doors of the big cupboard facing me slowly started to open.

CHAPTER TWELVE

1

I had the Smith-Wesson up as the doors gaped blankly. Something was coming out. Something like the hunched parody of a man with dark, staring eyes and a crumpled suit. The thin hair stood up like a spiky halo round the skull and the dried, blackened blood round the dead smile almost made my finger start pumping slugs.

The thing gave a long, wheezy sigh that sent my nerves to the ceiling and back and then buckled at the knees to land with a crash at my feet. I backed away instinctively and fanned the Smith-Wesson around until I had myself under control. It had been quite a moment.

I put the Smith-Wesson down again and lit a cigarette with a slightly unsteady hand, looking at the two scorched bullet holes in the chest that had punched the life out of old Harper. I had no doubt it was the tattoo artist I was looking at. The tips of his fingers were all stained with the various dyes he used in his craft.

I expelled blue smoke toward the ceiling, watching the light from the green blinds that remained pulled over a couple of the windows making little fretwork shadows over the staring eyes. Harper was a still life now right enough. And with his murder had gone all chances of nailing Jerry Freeman's killer.

Which was obviously why he'd been rubbed. I stooped to examine him, being careful where I put my hands. Then I straightened up and put the Smith-Wesson back in the holster. I wouldn't be needing it this afternoon. The old man had been dead for hours and the killer had obviously been long gone.

I searched around on the floor for any spent shells there might be. There weren't any but then I hadn't expected there to be. But it was best to make sure. There was a red plastic phone in the corner, near the work-bench and I went over with some vague idea of calling

McGiver. Then I thought better of it. I couldn't bring the police in without publicity and I didn't want Big Harry back before his time.

Best to present the facts to McGiver when I had something concrete. Maybe I could let him have the dye and the fragment of design without mentioning the Harper kill. I'd think of something. I went over to the cupboard, searched around for a while.

Harper's killer had stuffed the body in the cupboard but he'd omitted to close the catch properly; it was a big old iron thing and it had gradually eased into the open position with the pressure of the body. Otherwise I might have left without knowing about the kill. Question was had Big Harry taken him out? Or was I looking for someone else? I glanced at my watch. It was almost six now. It was time I got out. I didn't know whether Harper was married or had a housekeeper; I hadn't seen any evidence of feminine occupation of the premises but it was wise to leave before anyone came around. I needed a little more time. I had a couple of days yet before Rich would contact me. Though I wasn't sure where I was going from here. I'd think about that later.

I went through the studio, making sure I hadn't overlooked anything. I knew there wasn't much chance and it just made things more tough. There were still a lot of things I didn't know. Particularly why a wealthy oil executive with a beautiful wife would be mixed up with a society like the dragons. I stared grimly at the sprawled remains of Harper. He was the only man who could have told me.

I transferred my gaze through the window, made sure there was no-one around on the boulevard. Not that I could see very clearly but from here I had a view way down to the far end of the drive and on to a small section of road. The sun shone on blandly, the tree-tops waved in the breeze and it was the best of all possible worlds.

You're getting poetic again, Mike, I reminded myself. Though Candide wasn't exactly poetry. I stubbed out my cigarette on the back of my pack and put the butt back, made sure there was no trace of my presence here. Then I opened one of the windows for a couple of minutes to let the trace of tobacco smoke out. It was soon overlaid by the pungent odour of chemicals anyway.

I re-closed the window and door, using my handkerchief to brush away any trace of prints and went back downstairs. I'd already done the same to anything else I'd touched. Then, on impulse, I went in the living room and closed and locked the French doors. That would give me more time before Harper's body was found.

I wondered why the fragment of the dragon design had been left behind. Maybe someone was getting careless. Perhaps the killer had intended to tear it up and had then changed his mind, taking the design away with him, but overlooking the small fragment in the shadow of the bench.

It seemed highly likely. It had been a break for me but the dyes alone were conclusive. I knew now they'd match all right once the lab boys got on to testing them.

I went back to the front door and kept my eye on the drive. Nothing stirred in all the bright sunlight of that peaceful Southern Californian world. I caught the trace of a sardonic grin in the mirror opposite and suppressed it. Then I let myself quickly on to the stoop, dusting the door catch behind me and making sure it was secured with the automatic lock.

I went down the drive, my feet crunching in the gravel, feeling like I was in a spotlight, jumping every time the echo of my progress came back to me from the dense-packed mass of trees. I was in a lather of perspiration by the time I hit the road. Nothing moved in the sun-dazzle as I looked up and down its length.

I walked over to the Buick like I was treading on egg-shells. I hardly noticed the searing heat of the cushions as I got behind the wheel. I eased down the dusty road, idling the motor, trying not to make too much noise. I kept my self control until I got down near the bottom of the canyon.

Then I put my toe down and got the hell out.

2

'Why, Mike?' Stella said.

She stared at the bottle of red dye as it sparkled and shone on my blotter in the sunlight that came in from the blinds. I'd come in a little earlier this morning and it was still only nine-fifteen.

But I had a lot to do today and I wanted Stella's advice before I made my next move. A few ideas were stirring now but I needed a little stimulation to get the grey cells moving.

She saw the look in my eyes and smiled. She slipped off the edge of my desk and went over to put the percolator on. I seemed to have been drinking gallons of coffee on this case so far. Except for when I was being threatened or discovering corpses in cupboards.

Stella came back and went around to sit in the client's chair. She cupped her chin in her hands and stared at me with very blue eyes.

'Harper is the guy who did all the tattoos for this Red Dragon society, honey,' I said, answering her original question. 'He not only knew the people concerned but may have known about motives.'

Stella nodded slowly.

'Which would probably have identified the murderer.'

I eased back in my chair and shifted my glance on to the cracks in the ceiling.

'I guess Harper would have been taken out even if I hadn't been nosing around,' I said. 'The police would have gotten to him in the end. And the killer couldn't afford that.'

Stella shivered slightly.

'It's a horrible case altogether, Mike.'

I shrugged.

'Murder always is.'

Stella shook back the gold bell of her hair from her eyes.

'I didn't mean that, Mike. This society . . .'

'You shouldn't allow prejudice to cloud your judgement, honey. Faraday Investigations operates in the real world. We're at the gritty end.'

'It's a very nasty world,' Stella said.

'Sure,' I said. 'And Southern California's got a corner in every abnormality and sickness that afflicts mankind.'

Stella smiled faintly.

'Point taken, Professor. And spare me the lecture.

She went back to the alcove.

I waited until she returned, turning my head so I could admire her walk.

'So you're at a dead end again?'

I frowned.

'Looks like it.'

I sat back at the desk and stared in the direction of the stalled traffic on the boulevard.

'Yet there is a possibility,' I said.

Stella stirred in her chair.

'Such as.'

I grinned.

'All the leads usually come from you.'

'You're sparkling today,' Stella said severely.

'Something keeps nagging at the edges of my mind,' I said. 'It's the Jerry Freeman angle.'

Stella looked puzzled.

'But that's your whole case, Mike.'

'I know that,' I said. 'There's always been something phoney about it.'

I stared at the jar of red dye with the curious Chinese name and the fragment of glazed paper with the corner of the red dragon motif on it like they held all the answers to my problems.

'I was asked to investigate one murder,' I said. 'Now I got five. The others are getting in the way of the central problem.'

'I follow you to a certain extent,' Stella said in a far from convincing voice.

'We got a series of homosexual murders,' I said. 'Except that Jerry's wife—and the maid come to that—are convinced that he was a perfectly normal husband and partner. We got another interesting angle. That if he was a member of this club and was tattooed with the dragon design by means of this unique dye, it was done secretly and during the relatively short period he was away from his wife in the

108

Far East.'

'Where such tattoos are common,' Stella reminded me.

I gave her my grudging assent on that. Yet I had to go somewhere if I was to make any sense at all of the tangle. While I was still puzzling out loose ends Stella went back to refill my cup.

Come to think of it this case was all loose ends. There was a long silence in the office. The general gloom of my thoughts seemed to darken the brilliance of the sunshine at the window.

'I suppose there is no doubt at all that the dragon motif and the dye used will match up,' Stella said.

I stared at her for a long moment.

'I'm not quite with you.'

There was a faint smile at the corners of Stella's mouth now.

'You haven't been for years, Mike.'

I ignored that.

'I'm serious, honey.'

'And so am I,' Stella said. 'What I'm getting at is this. Supposing this man Harper did the dragon tattoo on Jerry Freeman and the other victims of these murders; that's one thing. But suppose the Freeman tattoo differs from that of the others, either in design or ink. What then?'

I stared at her for a moment longer.

'I'm listening,' I said.

'That would be a whole new ball game, Mike,' Stella said. 'I'm just throwing out suggestions.'

'And you're throwing them out good,' I said.

I nuzzled into my coffee cup again, digesting the new possibilities.

Then I looked at Stella grimly.

'There's only one way to find out.'

Stella looked at me with a startled expression.

'An exhumation order? Mrs Freeman would never agree.'

I shook my head stubbornly.

'We've got to try. An exhumation order and another autopsy. The police doctor probably didn't even examine that tattoo the first time around. He was dealing with a series of murders and there was no need to compare them in detail. Or so he thought.'

I shifted in my swivel chair. I was getting tired with all this gabbing.

'And then again the examinations might have been carried out by different surgeons. They had a pattern. They weren't looking for anything else.'

I stared at Stella reflectively.

'Like always, you've been a great help.'

I glanced down at the grounds in my coffee cup.

'I'm not looking forward to it but I'll go see Deirdre Freeman again after lunch. In the meantime I must keep my strength up.'

110

Stella smiled. She took the hint. She went back to the alcove to fetch me a third.

CHAPTER THIRTEEN

1

'Mr Faraday!'

Deirdre Freeman's face was chalk-white as she stared at me in the conservatory with its flowering shrubs and cloying atmosphere.

'You can't surely be serious?'

I looked at the vista of lawn and trees through the open doors. It was like a re-run of my first visit except that it was considerably more difficult.

'I can assure you I've never been more serious, Mrs Freeman.'

'But be reasonable, Mr Faraday. What good can it do to disturb the dead?'

It was Leo van Dorn this time, his clipped, distinguished voice filled with pain and alarm. His eyes softened as they sought those of his niece.

I stared from him to the girl Adele who stood midway between our small group in the cane chairs and the flowering screen of tropical plants which masked the door through which I'd come in. She had an agitated face and her hands were kneading and re-kneading

111

the front of her immaculate white apron.

'I'm not suggesting this for fun, Mr van Dorn,' I said. 'This business is deadly serious. I understand Mrs Freeman wanted me to find her husband's murderer. I can't do this without a second autopsy and I need your niece's permission for that.'

Deirdre Freeman raised an anguished face to mine. Today she wore a dark tailored suit which set off her figure in a striking way and her long, slim fingers were intertwined in her lap. For a second she performed the same agitated movements as the Filipino girl until she got herself under control again.

'But I cannot see what you possibly hope to achieve.'

'I agree, Mr Faraday,' said van Dorn.

He looked helplessly from me to the maid hovering in the background.

'Please don't think I'm trying to interfere. I have my niece's welfare solely at heart and I want only to avoid her further distress.'

I nodded.

'I quite understand that, Mr van Dorn. And I can assure you it's no pleasure to me to come here with such a request.'

The silver-haired man wore an immaculately cut business suit and his pale blue tie stood out crisply against his white shirt. There was the faint glint of a pin at the lapel of his jacket and for a moment I thought he resembled some benevolent Rotarian presiding at a business

112

conference.

'If you could only take us a little more into your confidence. Your reasons, for example. You haven't really told us why you make this strange request. If we knew, it might help us in coming to a decision.'

I shrugged.

'It's up to Mrs Freeman in the end, Mr van Dorn. If your niece won't play ball there's an end of it. But I understood she wanted to bring her husband's murderer to justice. She won't do that by closing her eyes to facts, however unpleasant.'

Deirdre Freeman flushed and stirred sharply in her chair like I'd just struck her across the face. I was playing pretty rough at that but if I wanted to get any farther forward I had to have her permission. A blunt approach was the only way of achieving that.

I hadn't forgotten Big Harry and the hitmen. They sounded like a pop group now I came to think of it. About half my time had run out. If I refused Rich's offer again the heavies would move in. Rich was my best bet. I knew I could make him crack regarding his client. Providing I knew who he was and where he lived. It was an impossible assignment from that point of view.

Freeman was my only way forward. Assuming I could ever get the drop on the big man and his companions they wouldn't tell me anything. And even if they did the trail wouldn't lead any farther back than Rich. He was the lawyer mouthpiece who was handling the hired help. With a great deal of distaste as I'd found out.

Van Dorn had half-risen from his chair, a heavy frown on his face.

'Come, Mr Faraday,' he said in an expostulatory voice. 'Aren't you being a little hard on Mrs Freeman. She's been through a great deal recently.'

I nodded.

'You're right, of course, Mr van Dorn. But I've got to play things the way I see them. If Mrs Freeman wants me off the case that's her prerogative.'

'No, no!' The girl had risen from her chair in an agitated way. 'I'm sure we can trust Mr Faraday, uncle. And we do want to get at the truth.'

The silver-haired man nodded.

'The decision is entirely yours, my dear. Naturally, I will defer to your wishes in the matter.'

He gave me a curt little inclination of the head and went on out, treading quietly like he was already in a funeral parlor. Adele was still hovering and her mistress looked at her distractedly. With her blonde, English-style beauty I had never felt Deirdre Freeman more appealing. Though this was no time for the romantic stuff.

'You may bring tea, Adele, when you are

114

ready.'

She smiled thinly.

'I think my uncle would prefer to take his in the study.'

She turned back to me as the maid left.

'You say this procedure is absolutely necessary, Mike?'

I nodded. She was dropping the formalities now that van Dorn was no longer present.

'If we're to get any farther forward.'

The girl came closer and put a small, cool hand in mine.

'Very well. You have my permission. I will be available to sign any papers the authorities may require.'

I looked at her steadily.

'Fine,' I said. I'll have things put in hand before the day's out.'

2

It was getting toward dusk when I arrived back at Police H.Q. There seemed to be a lot of activity going on and the entrance was thronged with pressmen and cameramen with expensive electronic flash-gear slung round their necks. I fought my way through to where the desk-sergeant was ensconsed. I knew him from way back and he shook his head, having to raise his voice to make himself heard clearly.

'There's a panic on, Mike. I don't know

exactly what. You want Homicide, I guess.'

I nodded.

'McGiver, actually.'

The Sergeant, a big, red-faced man called Rawlins slid off his stool and relinquished it to a perspiring red-haired young cop who looked nervously at the crowd milling around the other side of the desk. Rawlins drew me over to the water-cooler on the far side of the concourse, which was relatively clear.

He lowered his voice to a confidential whisper.

'Just had a buzz over the radio. McGiver's on his way back in. He should be hitting the car-park in about ten minutes.'

He grinned.

'You got a clear field. If you get there first. And providing the press boys don't get wind of it.'

'Thanks a lot,' I said.

I got back to the entrance again and made my way to the car-park, where I'd already slotted in the Buick. I sat in the driving seat, smoked a quick cigarette and watched the entrance. There was nobody else around except for a few cops who came and went with a purposeful air. No-one came near me.

In about five minutes a dark sedan showed. It seemed to be full of plain-clothes men. It crunched to a halt in a far corner of the lot. I got out the Buick and drifted on over before anyone could show.

116

McGiver was the third man out. He looked surprised, his face tired and haggard beneath the overhead lamps.

'Mike! You get your information quickly.'

I shook my head.

'I don't know what you're talking about. But the lobby's full of cameras and pressmen so I gathered there was something doing.'

McGiver made a wry face. He stopped and looked about him. He called over a tall, burly man with shoulders like a fullback.

'You'd better stall them off for an hour. I'll have a statement prepared later.'

'Right, Lieutenant.'

The other plain-clothes men melted away in different directions. McGiver looked at me expectantly.

'Let's sit in the car for a bit. I'm bushed.'

I offered him a cigarette and he took it with a grunt of satisfaction. I held the flame of the match for him, looking at the stubble on his face and chin. He looked like I felt on some of my rougher cases.

'It will be all in the papers tomorrow and on radio and TV tonight but I guess I can tell you. Your little lady can sleep nights from now on.'

I gave him a puzzled look.

'Stella?'

He shook his head, the corners of his mouth relaxing.

'No. I meant your client, Mrs Freeman.'

He couldn't keep the satisfied triumph of

the professional out of his eyes.

'We broke the case, Mike!'

'I wish you'd get to the point,' I said.

McGiver leaned forward in the car interior until his eyes were boring into mine.

'You must forgive my little touch of melodrama, Mike. We got the Red Dragon murderer!'

CHAPTER FOURTEEN

1

There was a long silence. I felt a distinct sense of anti-climax. The feeling that nothing was right on this case and would never be right sat like a sour taste in the pit of my stomach.

McGiver leaned over and tapped me on the knee.

'Of course, Mike, I can understand your disappointment. You wanted to crack the thing yourself. And then there's the question of your fee.'

I tried to keep the rising irritation out my voice.

'I didn't mean that at all,' I told McGiver. 'Sure, it's great news. And you deserve your moment of triumph. So what's the story?'

McGiver blew a thick cloud of smoke up toward the car roof, his eyes fixed on the faint red bars of sunset that still shone out beyond the glare of the floodlights in the parking concourse.

'We got lucky, that's all,' he said softly. 'It happens sometimes, even to us. The guy was a nutter. He rang us up to confess. Then, when we went out there to his house, he started to put the thing together for us. It fitted as to detail, as well as in general outline. A guy called Alan Ross. A wealthy businessman in his early sixties.'

The sour feeling in my stomach continued.

'I'm listening,' I said.

'He gave us stuff that only the murderer could have known,' McGiver went on reflectively. 'Then he became hysterical, started to retract. He went out in the bathroom and tried to commit suicide. He shot himself.'

I looked at McGiver in astonishment.

'And you let him.'

McGiver shifted uneasily in the dim light of the dashboard instruments.

'It wasn't like that, Mike,' he said defensively. 'This guy was all broken up. I thought he wanted to be sick.'

'And you hadn't searched him and didn't know he was carrying a cannon,' I said. 'An old hand like you. He was only a character who'd wasted a minimum of five people.'

McGiver rubbed his chin.

'It won't look good on my record,' he said

gloomily.

'What about my client's husband?' I said. 'Did he give you a rundown on the Freeman kill?'

McGiver looked defensive again.

'That was hardly the point, Mike. He was dealing with a series. Ross is in hospital with a bad gunshot wound. He may not make it. I'm not on your payroll, Mike. The Freeman kill was hardly the first thing that came to mind.'

'I'm sorry,' I said. 'I guess you've had a rough day.'

McGiver nodded slowly.

'Even for me,' he said.

I grinned.

'It goes with the badge,' I told him.

McGiver glanced at his watch.

'I've got to go see the Commissioner. Then I'll have the press on my neck. I'll fill the details in for you tomorrow.'

He reached over to the car radio, switched it on. There was a crackle and then a news flash came through. The announcer was having a field day with the Red Dragon kills. The names of Ross and McGiver were rattling around inside the car interior like a couple of billiard balls.

McGiver winced and flipped off the switch.

'What did I tell you?' he told the sunset.

I smiled again.

'The price of fame,' I said.

I got out the sedan and walked on over to

the Buick, leaving him there in the darkness and silence, gathering his frayed nerves together to meet the press.

I must have been anaesthetised with the impact of McGiver's news. I had no doubt that Ross was the man we both wanted. Or leastways, was the person responsible for the Red Dragon kills. And it wasn't just disappointment at not cracking the case myself.

There were things that didn't fit still. Principally because both Deirdre Freeman and the maid were so emphatic that Jerry Freeman had no homosexual connections. So there was an anomaly, the implications of which I was just beginning to grapple with.

I opened up the door of the Buick and slumped into the driving seat. I'd left it unlocked. It hardly seemed worth locking the car in here. That was my second major mistake of the evening.

A vast shadow stirred in the rear seat. The massive features of Big Harry stared at me in the mirror.

My scalded nerves re-arranged themselves back into their normal pattern.

'I didn't know it was Halloween yet,' I said.

Big Harry gravely inclined his head. He didn't break the ugly silence so I tried again.

'Mr Rich gave me three days,' I said. 'I've still got forty-eight hours.'

He shook his head.

'We had a change of plan,' he said. 'Circumstances alter cases.'

He moved so quickly I didn't stand a chance. I went out as definitively as silent movies.

2

When I came around a couple of goons with hob-nailed boots were dancing a tango on the rear of my skull and the floor of the automobile in which I was travelling kept advancing and receding in an alarming manner. I rolled over, felt my shoulder wedged. I reached for the Smith-Wesson, encountered only empty space.

The glutinous chuckle I'd heard once or twice before came over the heavy throb of the motor. The enormous face of Big Harry came into focus.

'Sorry I had to do that, Mr Faraday,' he said unemotionally. 'It saved a lot of time.'

I cleared my throat with difficulty, found I could speak.

'Oh, sure,' I said. 'I know how these things are.'

Big Harry reached down and dragged me effortlessly on to the passenger seat. I'd been lying doubled up in the space between the seat and the dashboard. I looked down incredulously. With my size and height I would have thought it physically impossible. It's amazing what you can achieve when you're relaxed, I told myself.

I sat quiet, waiting for my senses to come back, kept wishing the throbbing of my skull and the nausea would go away. I could see headlights in the mirror, following us in the darkness up the twisting road so I knew Big Harry's friends were in rear of us. Then I realised I was still in the Buick. There was no-one else. Like I said before there was no need.

Big Harry looked at me quickly. The Buick's a fairly big vehicle but he seemed to fill the entire space. Then he did a surprising thing. He handed me back the Smith-Wesson, barrel first. His strong teeth glinted in his wide mouth at my expression.

'I took the slugs out, of course. No need to put temptation in your way.'

'Of course,' I said.

I broke the pistol, just to make sure. The chambers were empty all right. I put the weapon back in my shoulder holster. My nerves had another jolt then. The barrel glanced against something before nuzzling into position. Memory came fully back.

I always keep a spare clip at the bottom of the holster. The big man hadn't thought to feel down in there. No reason for him to anyway. Assuming I had time to get to the gun and re-load, it might give me a chance. It could be vital because I had a feeling I might not be coming back from this trip.

'So where are we going?' I said.

The giant nodded to himself, expertly changing gear as we gunned up a steeper slope in the shadowy road. To our left the Pacific sparkled in the cloudy moonlight. The view didn't make me feel any better.

'A long ways,' he said softly.

'Sounds interesting,' I said.

The big guy glanced sharply through the windshield, like he was searching for a turn-off.

'I think you'll find it so.'

He looked at me reflectively. There was a faint hint of respect in his voice now.

'You're a pro, Mr Faraday. You won't make a fuss.

'I never have,' I told him modestly.

I half-turned in the seat, studying his face in the light from the instrument panel.

'I don't get the point of this. Or hadn't you heard. The Red Dragon killer has been found. He tried to commit suicide. He's in police custody, not expected to live.'

Big Harry shrugged.

'I don't know anything about that, Mr Faraday,' he said indifferently. 'I just follow orders. They come down from my principal.'

'Mr Rich?' I said.

There was a glint of amusement in his eyes.

'We both know better than that, Mr Faraday. He just transmits instructions. He's a cog like me.'

'A cog that's likely to break under pressure,' I said.

'That's none of my business,' he said. 'I shan't be around if anything goes wrong.'

'You can't hide your size,' I said. 'You should be pretty easy to trace. In Chicago or anywhere else for that matter.'

Big Harry gave his teeth another airing. The effect was bleak in the extreme.

'Don't worry about me, Mr Faraday. You just look after yourself.'

'I always try,' I said.

I asked him a question I'd had on my tongue for some minutes.

'Why did you give me the heater back?'

The big man spun the wheel and then we were bouncing down an overgrown side lane in the general direction of the sea.

'We like nice clean jobs. This is an accident, see. You're licensed to carry a gun. So if it's missing someone might get suspicious. If it's still in your holster that's nice and tidy.'

I gave Big Harry a battered grin.

'With no slugs?'

The big man shrugged again.

'Lots of operators carry unloaded shooters. They use them for effect only. Besides, you know as well as I do, private eyes don't often have cause to use them.'

'You have a point,' I said.

I glanced at the mirror again. We were on

bumpy ground now, travelling clear of thick clumps of trees and I could see the following headlights gyrating too as the sedan followed.

Big Harry grunted, slowing the car to a crawl.

'This is the end of the line,' he said, drawing up about two hundred yards from the cliff edge.

I had the passenger door open and hurled myself out before the Buick had finished rolling.

CHAPTER FIFTEEN

1

I landed badly, winded myself, almost passed out again. Big Harry had hit me harder than I thought. I heard his patient, pained voice over the throb of the Buick's motor before he switched it off. The car behind was accelerating up across the grass now. I hadn't much time.

'Don't make it hard for yourself, Mr Faraday. It only means we got to throw you over physically.'

I zig-zagged across the grass, making for the dark clump of trees. I had the Smith-Wesson out now, scrabbling with my finger-tips for the spare clip. The first shot came then, sending turf scattering about two yards behind me.

Big Harry shouted and no more shots came. He was using his head. He was dealing with an unarmed man who was to go over the cliff without physical damage. The three of them could hunt me down out here without any trouble. And if I'd been unarmed they could have done. Time was on Big Harry's side.

I was in darkness now but I could see the three men on the open turf in the pale moonlight. Even so three against one was too many. I decided to wait until they were in the dark too. I'd have an advantage then because my eyes were already accustomed to the light in here.

I moved over cautiously, treading carefully among the small branches that had fallen from the foliage overhead. The three men had scattered now. I kept my eye on the two gunsels but Big Harry was my prime target. I had to take him out. He was the one I feared most.

And all the while I snaked among the tree boles I knew I mustn't get too far away from the Buick. That was my only real chance of getting out of here with a whole skin. Assuming that the big man had left my keys in the ignition. I figured he might have done because they were three men against one unarmed person and because they were between me and the cliff.

If Big Harry planned to send me over in the

Buick he'd want the keys handy. All this was on the assumption I could keep clear of three big men who were all lethal pros. I had to choose right because there wouldn't be a second chance. There was just a slim possibility that the driver had left the keys in the sedan. But I wasn't banking on that.

I wasn't banking on the Buick really but I was playing for keeps tonight and my brain was ticking over sweetly. The three men were advancing across the open, keeping about ten yards apart, driving me toward the sea. Unless the cliff at my back was sheer here I might be able to outwit them.

I was still about ten yards from the cliff edge and soon I came across a tangle of boulders. I had an idea then. There was a rough path which skirted the boulders and I went down it, making sure it snaked along the cliff edge. It appeared to be sheer down below but the light was too poor for me to be sure.

I came back in rear of the rocks, found time to re-load the Smith-Wesson with none too steady fingers. Earlier on my head had been a little unreliable but the fresh air and the breeze blowing up here had cleared my brain.

Other thoughts were churning now, turning my mind in a certain direction. That sort of figuring would have to wait until later. Providing I came out all right. But I had the advantage, though the three men following so deliberately had no way of knowing.

I was up several feet from the ground now, in rear of the boulders. It was Big Harry I wanted and I could see through the thin black frieze of tree boles against the moonlight that he was dead centre, picking his way with deliberation across the grass. The other two men, one in a cream windbreaker and the second in a dark suit were out to left and right, some way off.

They didn't bother me for the moment. It was Big Harry, like I said. I felt a heel but it was him or me and he'd certainly marked me out for the mortuary slab. Sentimentality had no place in my business. I put the Smith-Wesson down on a rock at my right hand for a moment and scrabbled around, keeping as quiet as I could.

What I was looking for was something that would make a lot of noise. I found what I wanted after a few seconds and brought the sizeable boulder up next me, where I could use it in a hurry. I checked on the relative positions of the three men. They were still approximately the same as when I'd last seen them, except that they were appreciably nearer, of course.

Big Harry was about thirty feet off. I thought he seemed a little disconcerted that the terrain here didn't end in a sheer drop and he called out sharply to the other two to hurry. He came on at a steady pace, his hands empty so far as I could see. He had no suspicion that he was hunting anything other than a quarry which had no means of self-defence. Like I said he was a character who didn't need a gun.

The two men on the fringes had gone forward quickly and I could no longer see them as the trees had swallowed them up. That suited me fine. Big Harry had stopped now. He looked like an ebony statue silhouetted against the blue of the moonlight. He drew himself up and seemed to sniff the air.

Time stood still and I froze behind the rock, my face pressed close to the warm, gritty surface, listening to the thumping of my heart. It was so erratic it seemed like it might jump clear out of its mountings. I had the Smith-Wesson in my right hand, the loose boulder to my left now, where I could use it to the greatest advantage.

It depended which way the big man came. If he went to the left there was a sheer drop where I could take him out relatively silently, dropping the rock from a vertical position about twenty feet up. Even Big Harry couldn't survive that, providing my aim was good.

If he came the other way, following the path which looped in a shallow curve past the shelf where I was crouching, he would come behind me because the ground shelved steeply to where I was exposed on the sloping rock surface. In which case I should have to use the Smith-Wesson.

Big Harry cast his eyes around him and then made up his mind. He followed the shallow path that led to my right. I was already shifting over, leaving the rock where it was. I had the Smith-Wesson up high and wide as he came abreast of me behind a thin screen of bushes.

I rose up then and put two slugs in him. The explosions were so loud they seemed to blow a hole in the night.

2

Big Harry had an incredulous expression on his face as he stared at me. He took one step forward, clawed at the air with his hands and then fell over on his face. I went quickly back up to the rock. I had only three shells left and they had to last.

I'd heard shouting away to the right but now there was a deadly silence. That was the worst part of the night. I had two armed men, obviously converging on the place where I was concealed. I quickly took hold of the boulder. I had another idea then.

I gave myself a twisted smile, more for morale than anything else. I wasn't thinking good. I was looking at the situation from my point of view, not theirs. So far as they were concerned Big Harry had shot at something, probably the unarmed fugitive, with his own weapon. So far as I knew they didn't even know what I looked like.

But in any event, though they were obviously converging on the boulders fast, they wouldn't be alarmed; they were still chasing a defenceless man. So I still had the drop on them. I put the Smith-Wesson down again, my mouth harsh and dry, with a bitter taste of fear way down inside me. But I was thinking good and doing all the right things for the moment.

I moved over to the boulder, put it where it would be ready to roll. All I had to do now was wait. I could already hear someone coming from the left. I strained my eyes up toward the tree-line, hearing for the first time the soft murmur of the Pacific at my back. Maybe the breeze had changed or something. Not that it mattered a lot. It was just one of those things a character in my position noticed and assessed automatically.

For the first time I saw the dark silhouettes of the Buick and the hitmens' sedan standing in the middle of the field; they looked like the blurred images of cattle browsing there. I measured the distance between myself and the Buick. It seemed impossibly far. I couldn't hear anything from the right for the moment.

Maybe the second man, the one in the dark suit, had gone down another path and was working his way across the shoulder of hillside. That left the first man, the one in the grey windcheater, who would most likely arrive ahead of the other, from the left.

It was important to know these things. The

man in grey would stand out more easily in the moonlight and make a better target. Whereas the man in the dark suit, if he stayed in the deep shadow of the trees, would be very difficult to pick out. Like always I'd have to play it by ear. It depended on which man arrived first.

I'd been there perhaps another five minutes, straining my ears, when I heard a slithering sound about fifty yards to my left. It would be grey windcheater then. Which made things a little easier.

A few seconds later I saw him, coming along the tree-line, clear-minted in the moonlight. He was holding a big cannon casually in his left hand, not looking particularly worried or concerned. Like I figured he thought he knew the score. I flattened myself behind the boulders, waiting for him to close the range.

There was no point in loosing off too soon. I had little or no chance of hitting him among the trees and the trunks would probably deflect or absorb the shots. A twig snapped in the silence then and I could feel sweat trickling down my cheek in the warmth of the night.

When I raised my head again I couldn't see him for a moment. I glanced at my watch quickly. Five or ten minutes only had passed since I'd taken out Big Harry. It seemed like five years on the time-scale in which I was living. I heard another furtive movement then and glanced up quickly.

I could hear a scraping noise caused by heavy boots on a dry rock surface. Almost too late I realised the man in the grey windcheater was climbing up toward me without bothering to go around by the path. He probably only wanted to get a better view from the top of the boulders but it was nearly fatal in my case.

I raised my head just in time to see him appear over the rim. His reflexes were as quick as a cat's. The force of the explosion stunned my senses. I rolled over as the big slug chipped pieces out of the rock surface a foot from me. He was shooting instinctively, without proper aim.

My own response was equally impromptu but I was at rest now, shooting upward against the big man's silhouette. The two explosions followed the first so closely they seemed like echoes. One would have done but I couldn't control my reflexes. It was understandable in the circumstances.

The man in the grey windcheater was blown away before he reached my level. I saw his open mouth a black O in the whiteness of his face, the cannon already in the air. He went down and out of sight in a crackle of undergrowth. There was another rustling to the right as I got to the boulder on the slab beside me.

That would be the man in the dark suit. I gave a hoarse cry and levered the boulder off the rock. It went crashing and tearing through the undergrowth on its way down the hillside. It sounded pretty good to me. A gun flamed then in the darkness of the trees.

I was crouched down but the shot wasn't aimed at me. It spanged off a tree-trunk somewhere toward the cliff edge as the rock went on rolling. I could hear crashing noises then as the big man set off in pursuit. I got down off the boulders, stepping round the body of the man in the windcheater. He didn't move and I had no time to waste on him.

I crouched low and picked my way with care toward the edge of the trees. Then I had my arms tucked into my sides and was zig-zagging back toward the Buick in the moonlight. I felt cold and exposed out here but there was no sound from the darkness of the trees I'd left behind me.

My heart was thumping like crazy in my rib-cage and my breath sobbing in my throat when I got up to the Buick. I ignored the sedan. What I ought to do was to rip the wires to the distributor head. But that meant I could be caught out here in the open. And the man in the dark suit wouldn't miss, shooting from the shadow at the edge of the meadow.

I opened up the Buick driving door, keeping low. I remembered then that the man in the grey windcheater might have been the driver of the sedan. If he was then he'd most probably have the ignition keys in his pocket. In which case the second gunsel would have to

135

go back for them if he wanted to use the sedan.

Which would give me plenty of time. My heart jumped as I caught a glint of metal at the ignition. Big Harry had left the keys in when I'd dived out the car. I got behind the wheel and closed the driving door as a dark figure broke cover at the edge of the tree-line. I fired the motor. It started first pull because it was still warm from the drive out. The noise covered the gunsel's shot but I could see a flicker of flame at the tree-edge.

I had my toe down now and was tearing up turf as I put the Buick round in a screaming circle. I steadied up as the dark man came pounding across the field toward me, his big cannon held wide and high. I got my last shot off then from the open driving window and had the satisfaction of seeing him go flat on the grass.

Then I had straightened up and put the Buick, bucking and rocking like a mad thing, over the rough terrain and back on to the secondary lane. A minute later I was out on metalled roadway and putting mileage between me and the dark-suited man on my way back into town.

CHAPTER SIXTEEN

1

'Why an autopsy, Mike?'

McGiver repeated the question for the third time, his dark-rimmed eyes looking grimly at me across the surface of his battered old desk. It was eleven o'clock now but I'd found him still on duty at Police H.Q., as I'd expected him to be.

I hadn't told him about the shoot-out yet. I'd leave that until a little later. He still had a lot on his mind. I sat back in the chair in front of his desk and swilled my second coffee in the paper cup from the automatic dispensing machine in the corridor outside. It wasn't bad for such a brew.

Unless I was being uncritical in my reaction after the night's events.

'Because there's something different about the Freeman kill from the others,' I said.

McGiver scratched his already rumpled hair.

'Give me examples.'

'For one thing Freeman wasn't a homosexual,' I said. 'The medical evidence you've just shown me proves that.'

McGiver looked uneasy.

'I give you that, Mike.'

'And now you tell me that the gun which killed Freeman is different to that used by Ross. Which proves something.'

'You have a point,' McGiver said slowly. 'But what is all this leading up to?'

'It's just a hunch,' I told him. 'Ross died an hour ago, right? So you won't be getting any information from that quarter. The rest of the Red Dragon kills match up to his pistol according to your ballistics people. So we haven't got the murder weapon in Freeman's case.'

'You mean our police surgeons missed something on the Freeman kill?'

I shook my head.

'I don't know. Maybe they were looking at the wrong things. It's possible. There's another reason too. One that reinforces my theory.'

McGiver sat up quickly.

'The hell they did.'

I stopped him from going on.

'We'll go into all that later. There's a significant factor which other things drove out of my mind. Now I've had time to think and it's cast-iron fact.'

'Get to the point, Mike,' McGiver said irritably.

I didn't blame him. A man without sleep and driven incessantly gets edgy, sometimes without good reason.

'Ross confessed to the Dragon kills,' I said. 'It was on the radio tonight and splashed

138

around in the late editions.'

'So what?' McGiver said.

'So this,' I told him. 'That wrapped up the case. So far as the dragons were concerned. But it made no difference to the people out to get me. They had their orders. I was on the Freeman kill. The man responsible for that didn't want any more evidence turned up. He probably guessed I was stalling for time.'

McGiver's eyes had a strange light in them. All the tiredness seemed to drop away from him.

'All right, Mike. I'll buy it. I think you're on to something. But what about Mrs Freeman?'

'I already told you about that,' I said. 'She's agreed. Just send the papers over and she'll sign them.'

McGiver nodded.

'I'll give you a ring tomorrow, Mike.'

I shook my head.

'Let's do it tonight, Mac. We can send the papers over for signing in the morning.'

McGiver gave me one of his long, hard looks.

'This could mean my badge, Mike. And my pension.'

I grinned.

'The hell with your badge and your pension both. Let's get this cracked. Freeman was killed for a purpose. Maybe his killer will strike again.'

McGiver shrugged, his face serious.

139

'The hell with my badge, like you say. Your licence is on the line as well.'

'That goes without saying,' I told him.

McGiver pulled the phone toward him.

'I'll get some people on to it,' he said. 'Where did you say he was buried?'

2

It was quiet in the mortuary office. The big clock screwed to the wall over the mahogany double doors showed a few minutes after three a.m. It was that dead time when everything seemed asleep. No puns intended. McGiver stirred on the hard bench opposite and opened one eye.

'Anything happening?'

I shook my head.

'Give them time.'

He shrugged.

'It's been over two hours. Doc Rodmeyer is usually much quicker than this. And as you specified a tattoo specialist . . .'

He sat up quickly.

'You realise how much this is costing the County?'

'Relax,' I said. 'It won't be long now. We wanted definitive and incontrovertible proof, didn't we. And he's got to match up that dye I gave him. He's analysing that first.'

McGiver glanced at the bored patrolman who was slumped in a wooden chair up near the door.

'I guess you're right, Mike. It's just that I've got so much other stuff hanging round my neck.'

'You'll be getting a couple week's leave when this is over,' I said.

McGiver looked at me incredulously.

'That'll be the day,' he said.

We were still waiting there like that when the door opened and a man in a white surgeon's smock, smeared and discoloured, and wearing white rubber gloves came in. He held a sheaf of papers in his hands and he had an air of suppressed excitement.

'We got something, gentlemen!'

He turned to me.

'Your hunch was right, Mr Faraday.'

McGiver got up too but Rodmeyer held out his hand and put the papers down on a corner of his desk. He was a tall, elderly man with a thick silver mustache which softened the severity of the heavy lines which made deep grooves at the corners of his mouth. His matching silver hair shone in the overhead lamplight as he stripped off his gloves at a basin in a corner of the big office.

'If you'll just give me a moment to scrub up, gentlemen, I'll be with you.'

McGiver went over to the desk, fingering the sheaf of documents on the heavy clipboard with suppressed curiosity. Rodmeyer was back now, towelling his hands briskly. He'd stripped off the gown and was in his shirt-sleeves. He went around to sit in back of the desk.

He gestured to a worktop near the sink.

'There's a percolator and cups there if someone would like to pour. It looks like being a hard night. And I guess your officer could use a cup.'

The big cop at the door rose gratefully and went across to the worktop. When we were settled round the desk McGiver looked at the big, lean doctor expectantly. Rodmeyer addressed himself to me first.

'I'm obliged to you, Mr Faraday, for pointing me in this direction. That dye was quite unique. We still don't know all its chemical constituents.'

He pursed his lips.

'And that's unusual because I've made a study of tattoos and related matters.'

'A very clever little man was responsible,' I said. 'A retired tattoo artist who still carried out a lot of private work. He did the Red Dragon tattoos for this society Ross was so busy eliminating. And I'm certain he also did the one on Jerry Freeman.'

'There's something very interesting about that,' the doc began when McGiver interrupted.

'You never told me anything about this tattoo character,' he said suspiciously.

'I must have forgotten,' I said. 'He's called Lou Harper. He's lying dead in the attic of his house over at 1122 Romero Drive. The place is got up as a tattoo parlor. Someone had chilled him with a pistol and stuffed him in a cupboard.'

McGiver gave a harsh sigh in the cloying silence of the office.

'That's something else you forgot to tell me,' he said bitterly.

'I would have gotten around to it,' I said. 'I've been rather busy lately.'

Rodmeyer gave me a quick, bleak smile.

'Let's get back to the matter in hand, Lieutenant,' he said mildly. 'We don't want to be here all night and my time is rather precious.'

'Of course, doc,' McGiver said quickly. 'But I'd like Mr Faraday here to give me a list of hits he's seen around town before we leave the office. I like to run a nice tidy bureau.'

'Sure,' I said. 'Anything to oblige.'

Rodmeyer rustled his sheaf of papers.

'Here's how I see it, gentlemen,' he said crisply. 'Freeman was shot, of course, as you already know, but the bullet doesn't match the riflings already found in the other cases. It came from another gun altogether. That's old history.'

He shuffled the papers again.

'But Mr Faraday directed us to an altogether different area. And I found something very interesting about that Red Dragon tattoo.'

He leaned forward across the desk, his eyes alight with excitement.

143

'Except that it wasn't a tattoo at all.'

There was a heavy silence in the office, broken only by the big squadman going over to pour himself another cup of coffee. The tall doctor was obviously pleased with the impression he'd created.

'Then why didn't the pathologist who did the original autopsy pick it up?' McGiver asked.

'He wasn't asked to examine the tattoo specifically. He was dealing with gunshot wounds, cause of death, that sort of thing. And that red dragon photographed exactly the same as the others because it had been done by the same artist. And the man was an artist, there's no doubt about that.'

'What are you trying to tell us, doc?' McGiver said heavily.

Rodmeyer took another gulp of his coffee, put the cup down on a sheaf of reports.

'It was very cleverly done. Beautifully done, in fact. In another context it might be called a masterpiece of trompe l'oeil.'

McGiver screwed up his face.

'Come off it, doc,' he complained. 'Keep it to English. Faraday's theories are hard enough to stomach in any case.'

The doctor grinned at me.

'What I'm trying to say is this. That tattoo wasn't a tattoo, like I said.'

'Well, what was it?' McGiver broke in impatiently.

Wheels were starting to turn in my head now. Slowly, it's true, but they were on the move. I got up to re-fill my cup, took Rodmeyer's as well. He'd earned another. There was a smouldering silence in the office as I went back to the desk and sat down again. McGiver waited, his eyes bleak, but he was restraining his impatience well. Rodmeyer was pleased. I didn't want to deny him his little theatrical effects.

'Where did that dye you found come from, Mr Faraday?' he said.

I shrugged.

'I'm no expert. Harper's place latterly. My guess is the Far East initially. I understand it's special.'

Rodmeyer shifted in his chair, cupping his hands round his coffee cup.

'It's special all right,' he said crisply. 'In fact it's very special. Not only in its brilliant and unusual shade. It has another property too.'

'What property?' McGiver said.

'The dragon mark had been drawn on to Freeman's skin, using something like a very fine steel-nibbed pen. It wasn't a tattoo but it had been done so cleverly and skilfully that it would take an expert to detect it.'

McGiver was sitting up straight in his chair now. He stared at me without saying anything.

'That tattoo won't wash off. I've tried it with every known chemical but I can't remove it,' Doc Rodmeyer went on. 'Which makes it not exactly unique but virtually so.'

'So the pathologist wouldn't have been able to remove it when the body was washed and laid out,' McGiver said quickly.

Rodmeyer turned his eyes toward the ceiling.

'That's what I just said,' he complained.

'There was something else, wasn't there?' I said.

The doctor nodded slowly.

'You're a very percipient man, Mr Faraday.'

'Not really,' I said. 'But it's my case. I've been retained by Jerry Freeman's widow. So I've concentrated on this one thing. I've been blind until now.'

'You haven't heard it all yet,' Rodmeyer went on. 'This so-called tattoo was unique in another respect.'

I felt a slight tingling of the scalp. It's something I get very rarely. Perhaps when a strongly felt hunch is crystallising. That moment was fast approaching now.

Rodmeyer fixed the big uniformed officer with his best professional stare, then switched his gaze to the Lieutenant and finally to me.

'That Red Dragon motif was painted on to Freeman's skin after he was dead,' he said.

CHAPTER SEVENTEEN

1

'So you were right, Mike?'

Stella's face was concerned as she stared at me across the desk. It was almost midday now and I'd gone home for a few hours' shut-eye and to re-load the Smith-Wesson. I hadn't forgotten the gunsel in black. There was most likely a contract still out on me and I'd kept my eyes peeled all the way across town.

'Partly by accident,' I said.

I felt the lump at the back of my skull. It was coming up nicely now. Stella shivered slightly as she caught the movement. She went back to the alcove to bring me a second cup.

'Richter rang in,' she said. 'To warn you about Big Harry being a Chicago pro. He said he was dangerous.'

'Thanks a lot,' I said.

Stella gave me a faint smile.

'Everything begins to fit beautifully now,' I said. 'A very clever mind which worked a brilliant scheme.'

Stella went to sit in the client's chair, keeping her eyes on my face. Today she wore a white dress with a flared skirt that set off her figure in great style. The material of the dress had large buttons and little red flower motifs on it which seemed to ripple and sway in the breeze whenever Stella walked. That glittering was taking me quite a lot this morning. If you know what I mean.

'What scheme, Mike?'

'It was staring me right in the face all the time,' I said. 'I couldn't quite work it out but I told you that the Freeman kill didn't sit right.'

'I remember,' Stella said.

She leaned forward to cup her chin on her hands.

'Someone had a marvellous murder scheme that was so simple it would have passed unnoticed,' I went on. 'There was only one snag and that was the murder weapon wouldn't match. But the killer still thought it would pass. He simply camouflaged the kill by dropping it in the middle of the Red Dragon series.'

'By having Harper draw the motif on Freeman's corpse after he'd killed him,' Stella said.

I nodded.

'Which meant Harper knew the identity of the killer. So he had to die before I could question him.'

Stella took a delicate little sip of her coffee.

'I take it money would be the motive?' she said.

I leaned back in my old swivel chair and stared at the cracks in the ceiling. My headache was receding into the background

148

now.

'Too right, honey,' I said. 'There may be three to five million dollars involved. Freeman was an oil millionaire though he kept a low profile so far as those people go.'

'So who's the beneficiary?' Stella said softly.

I gave her one of my bland looks.

'Mrs Freeman inherits,' I said. 'I haven't gone into that angle too deeply yet.'

'I'll bet,' Stella said.

'There's another important point,' I said. 'Whoever knocked over Freeman is pretty good at covering his tracks. He—or she—probably met Freeman at the airport and drove home with him.'

Stella nodded.

'It was a hire car, remember.'

'I remember,' I told her. 'Probably booked in Freeman's name. So the body was taken away, perhaps to Harper's workshop or somewhere else nearby. Then undressed and worked on prior to being returned to the place where the vehicle was parked. Before rigor mortis set in.'

Stella shivered again.

'The most important thing was last night,' I said. 'The killer decided to have me taken out by his hit-squad after Ross had confessed to the Red Dragon murders. Which meant he couldn't afford to have me nosing around the Freeman kill any longer.'

'Or she,' Stella reminded me.

She leaned forward and drained her cup.

'Still, you haven't got much farther to go. As Mrs Freeman is the beneficiary ...'

'It's getting something to break,' I said. 'I'm almost there but I need the link. There's one gunsel still loose and he won't give up.'

Stella's eyes were pinned to mine now.

'There's still your Mr Rich,' she said.

'He's just a stooge,' I said. 'Probably a corporation lawyer.'

'But he may give you a direct link,' Stella persisted.

'It's worth a try.'

She looked at me critically.

'And hadn't you better report to your client?' she said gently. 'After last night's fuss she'll want to know what the score is.'

Like always, Stella was talking sense.

'You'd better see if you can reach her,' I told her.

I wasn't looking forward to the interview. Stella gave me a tight smile and reached out for the phone.

2

The Onoco Corporation Building was and is a powerful pile of chrome, marble, steel and concrete on a main boulevard location. It was early afternoon when I got over there and the heat was oppressive and enervating. Mrs Freeman hadn't been home when Stella had reached the house and I'd spoken to Adele instead.

She'd said her mistress had some business at Onoco and I could be sure to find her between three and four p.m. Seemed like Deirdre Freeman was on the wing; maybe to avoid awkward questions my end. I remembered the look on Stella's face when she'd spoken of the legacy and my suspicions came flooding back. Several million dollars was a big temptation but I had to walk very carefully here.

Somehow I had to tie in Big Harry and his squad and the nervous Mr Rich, assuming I could ever find him again. It was a large order and I mulled it over for a while as I drove, my brain cogs turning sluggishly again but all the time I never forgot to keep my eyes on the rear mirror. I was beginning to feel like a Battle of Britain pilot in September 1940 by the time I tooled the Buick into a vacant space in the parking lot belonging to the Onoco Corporation.

I went on in over the vast concourse with its marble flags and discreet walnut panelled decor. I could see from the plaques screwed to the walls that the Onoco Corporation dealt with a great many commodities and that it was somehow linked to the New York stock market. Not that I'm an expert on such things.

But I was impressed even before I got up to the enormous reception desk that was like something out of Goering's study at Karinhall.

Or maybe it was Carinhall. I couldn't remember at this distance in time. A tall, blonde number whose hair was shining like it was a brilliantly burnished copper helmet was buffing her nails and looking like she was Michaelangelo working on The Last Supper. Or something about that price-range.

When she condescended to notice my presence I had to trade glances with her for half a minute before I could persuade her to drag her expensive underwear over in my direction. The lips parted in a half-smile.

'Yes?'

'I'd like to see Mrs Deirdre Freeman,' I said. 'I understand she's visiting here this afternoon.'

The blonde number ran a scarlet fingernail down an expensive-looking leather-bound appointments book.

'Oh, yes. But you'll have to wait. She's in with the President.'

'That's all right,' I said. 'I presume it's in order to go on up.'

The blonde girl hesitated, looking beyond me to where a uniformed security guard hovered uneasily.

'You a friend of Mrs Freeman?' she said.

I gave her one of my pleasant expressions.

'That's right.'

She nodded and became brisk, scribbling something on a printed form.

'I'll just get you to sign this.'

152

I dashed my signature off at the bottom. 'Just a matter of form,' I said. The tall number didn't even crack a half-millimetre smile. I remembered Mr Pooter and his wry remark about the draper's assistant having no sense of humour. I knew how he felt for a moment or two.

'Just take the elevator to the fourteenth floor,' the girl said. 'Then follow the arrows to the President's Suite.'

I began to feel like I was at the court of Ronnie Reagan but I thanked her anyway and wheeled on over to the elevator cages at the far side of the concourse.

An elevator boy with more braid on him than Marshal Timoshenko during the Russian campaign whirled me up fourteen floors to what looked like a ritzier section of the New York Hilton.

There was a cluster of illuminated notices screwed to the wall of the corridor opposite, with arrows directing the visitor to various suites. I could hear typewriters and electronic equipment mumbling behind some of the doors of the suites, many of which had glass walls.

I gathered the President's quarters were to the left, up at the far end but before I got there I came to a circular concourse with concealed lighting from the ceiling throwing a bland radiance down on to polished brown leather banquettes formed in a circle with four

153

openings corresponding to the angles of the intersecting corridors.

There was an ornamental fountain in the centre with the jets actually playing and huge fish with faces like elongated versions of Edward G. Robinson that champed their jaws and swam sadly between ornamental greenery. But the jets gave a fresh atmosphere to the place and I skirted the vast beaten copper bowl in which the fountain basin was sheathed and sat down at the end of one of the divans.

There was no-one else around but plenty of magazines and I picked one up, watching from over the top the section of corridor where I guessed Deirdre Freeman would show when her interview was over. I never got that far with the scenario though.

There was an office almost opposite where I was sitting which had a legend stencilled in gold letters on the wooden panelling. It said; J.R. Witherspoon. Assistant to the President. A familiar figure with a worried face was pacing about behind the clear glass of the office area. I froze in my seat and buried myself in the magazine.

A few moments later the door opened and the man came out. I looked cautiously beyond the journal, keeping my face hidden. There was no mistaking the character. The nervous manner, the haunted eyes, the bald head and pebble glasses, the mustache, even the clothing was the same.

Mr Rich, the employer of gunsels, the holder-out of envelopes with five thousand dollar bonuses, master of the nervous tic, turned to the right and went along the corridor to the elevator cages. I got up quickly, all thought of Deirdre Freeman forgotten, and followed.

CHAPTER EIGHTEEN

1

I kept behind the angle of the concourse, easing cautiously round until I could see down the far end of the corridor. Witherspoon had his back to me, waiting for an elevator cage to come up. He was studying some papers in his hand, his head bent. I could see by the indicator lights high up on the wall that two elevators were on their way.

I hoped I'd be able to catch another to get me to the ground floor in time to pick up my man again. I didn't know he was leaving the building, of course, but I had to get down if I wanted to follow him and the ground floor was obviously the best place.

There was a lot of space and plenty of people there and I could observe without being seen. And if I missed him I'd find some way of getting his private address at the desk. I could probably achieve the same objective by checking the phone book but he could be ex-directory. A lot of these well-heeled executives were. I knew there was a lot of TV surveillance in here so I merely feigned a casual curiosity and went back to put my magazine on the table.

The elevator stopped at the fourteenth while I was doing that and I got back to the corridor intersection just in time to see Witherspoon step in. There were four cages here and they were starting to get busy. Another stopped ten seconds later on its way down and I piled in. This one was automatic and I buttoned the ground floor, leaving my stomach up in the Presidential Suite as the polished wood cage plunged downward.

I picked Witherspoon up without trouble in the concourse. He didn't seem in any hurry and he'd stopped for a chat with the blonde girl at the reception desk. He seemed to be checking on some mail and I hung around in the lobby and studied one of the notice boards.

If he was Witherspoon, of course. He could have just been visiting. But it was too much of a coincidence. If he wasn't Witherspoon he certainly worked in the building. As he detached himself and went slowly toward the main doors, sifting his mail, I drifted over to the desk.

'I was told Mr Witherspoon just came down,' I said. 'You remember me. I was asking about Mrs Freeman.'

'Oh, yes, Mr Faraday. You just missed Mr Witherspoon.'

She jerked a scarlet-nailed forefinger over toward the main doors.

'He left. But if you hurry you'll be able to catch him up in the car-park.'

'Thanks,' I said.

I hurried on out like I was anxious to find him. I was two points ahead of the game. My man was Witherspoon and so I could pick him up at the Onoco Corporation any time. And he was going to the car-park. Which gave me a chance to get to the Buick. I spotted the nervous character with the pebble glasses almost immediately. He had opened one or two letters and was scanning them anxiously, like they contained bad news. I hadn't forgotten the man in the dark suit and I kept my eyes peeled as I made for the parking area, taking care to give Witherspoon a wide sweep. He had his back to me in any case.

If Witherspoon didn't lead me to the man I wanted this afternoon at least I felt pretty confident I could shake the information out of him. The sun was a little lower in the sky but it was still pretty hot and I felt sweat damp on my shoulder-blades as I hurried down the aisles between the parked cars, the Smith-Wesson making a reassuring pressure against my chest muscles.

I'd re-loaded the chambers, of course, and I

had the spare clip in my jacket pocket just in case the man who'd killed Jerry Freeman came up with any more surprises. Or the woman who'd killed him. I hadn't forgotten my conversation with Stella yesterday.

I didn't know where Witherspoon was parked so I got in the Buick quickly, winding down the windows to let out the heat and idled on down toward the entrance. My man went by a couple of minutes later, his head bent over the wheel, eyes straight ahead as he drifted up toward the entrance leading to the main boulevard.

He was driving a white Pontiac so he wouldn't be very hard to keep in view. He eased out into the traffic stream, turning to the right. I slotted in, keeping two cars behind, like I usually do when I'm tailing. We started making time across town.

2

It was about half an hour's steady ride to where we were going and I drove on down the boulevard, noting where Witherspoon had turned in to the driveway of a fairly substantial house behind a screen of ornamental trees, including some particularly fine jacarandas. But I wasn't here for the gardening notes and I went on down, looking for a slot to park.

There were a lot of vehicles in here; maybe someone was giving an afternoon bunfight. It was that sort of chintzy area, with striped sunshades and cane furniture on the front lawns and even a couple of good-looking people on a flowered canvas swing like they were Scott and Zelda preparing for a heavy evening's drinking.

I looked for Gatsby making his way across the lawn but he didn't seem to be home this afternoon. I had to park about two hundred yards from Witherspoon's place in the end and I padded on down toward his driveway, the sun hot on my head, my brain still buzzing with half-formulated thoughts. I had another appointment with McGiver later this evening. And a lot of explaining to do. I wanted to get my story straight before then.

I needed to get the case straight before then, come to that. It would look better on my record as well as McGiver's. I drifted past the drive I wanted, noting the white automobile in front of the steps. There didn't seem to be anyone else around. I got in the entrance quickly and walked up on to the lawn bordering it. That way the trees screened me until I was almost at the house.

There was a zig-zag crazy path that led away from the front and I followed it in rear, hearing faint music coming from behind the Japanese paper blinds. The windows were already open, letting in the late afternoon breeze and the place would have made a nice colour supplement. Except that I wasn't here for that either.

I went up on the stoop at what I figured might be the kitchen entrance and buttoned the bell. The door was opened almost immediately by Witherspoon. He was already in his shirt-sleeves, his worried face glazed with sweat, his eyes blinking behind the pebble glasses, a freshly-opened can of iced beer in his right hand. He almost dropped the beer when he recognised me, and his face worked convulsively before he found his voice.

'Mr Faraday! I certainly didn't expect you.'

'I'll bet,' I said.

I eased past him into the big tiled kitchen with its gleaming steel fittings, looking around carefully.

'You married?' I said. 'Anyone else here?'

Witherspoon shook his head mournfully, slamming and bolting the kitchen door behind us.

'I was once,' he said in a dull voice. 'It didn't take. I have a housekeeper who comes in several times a week. She's already been today.'

I nodded.

'Good. Then we can talk.'

Witherspoon took a sip of the beer like it would steady his nerves. He bit his lip and squared his narrow shoulders.

'Look, Mr Faraday,' he began. 'I know what you must think. I was just following orders. I was going to contact you but the three days

160

isn't up yet . . .'

I interrupted him.

'I'm not interested in that. Those goons of yours didn't wait. They jumped the gun, tried to kill me. Two of them are dead now. I don't want the third around my neck.'

Witherspoon gave a strangled snort and his face turned an alarming ashen colour. He took an unsteady step forward, his eyes wide and haunted. He put the empty beer can down very deliberately on one of the stainless steel draining boards, the metallic clatter eating at my nerves.

'My God, Mr Faraday, you don't think I had anything to do with that? My principal said those people were there just in case of trouble. You don't think I'm mixed up in this.'

'Up to your sweet neck,' I said. 'And it's your principal I'm interested in.'

Witherspoon licked dry lips and looked desperately around the kitchen.

'Good heavens, Mr Faraday, we may both be in grave danger.'

I gave him a crooked grin.

'You astonish me, Mr Witherspoon. I want that name.'

Witherspoon put his hand up quickly and bent his head on one side as though listening for some sound I couldn't hear.

'It would be more than my job is worth, Mr Faraday,' he said in a tremulous voice.

I shook my head.

'It will be more than your life is worth if you don't come clean.'

Witherspoon's face was changing colour again. He was getting more like a traffic signal by the minute.

'You don't understand, Mr Faraday. You don't want me. I was just transmitting a message. I had no idea what was involved.'

'That's what they all say,' I told him.

I got out the Smith-Wesson and held it up in front of his shocked face.

'I'm a peaceable guy,' I said. 'Except when I'm shot at and people try to murder me. You're part of this pattern. So you got to take responsibility. And expect nasty things to happen to you.'

He licked his lips again. His voice was so low and trembly I had a job to make out what he was saying.

'I don't understand, Mr Faraday. What do you mean?'

'Just this,' I said. 'If I don't get the information I came here for I'm going to take you apart, piece by piece.'

His eyes were sick now. I almost felt sorry for him but I had to go on.

'What do you want to know?'

'Everything,' I told him. 'Firstly, who were those gunsels?'

He shook his head vehemently.

'That wasn't my end, Mr Faraday. I was merely given my instructions. I didn't know they were going to be like that. I was as shocked as you were.'

I shrugged.

'I'll buy that. Go on.'

Witherspoon put a shaking hand up inside his collar, looking round the kitchen worriedly. The paper blinds that were filtering the strong sunlight shifted and rattled in the breeze, like there were people outside trying to get in. The noise was getting on my nerves a little too.

'How did you trace me, Mr Faraday?'

'By accident,' I said. 'I'm asking the questions. But there's no reason you shouldn't know. I was visiting the Onoco Corporation building today looking for my client. I saw you come out of your office and recognised you. I followed you here. That's all.'

Witherspoon nodded, opening his mouth. I saw his eyes glaze again and then widen with fear. I whirled as the first explosion seemed to shatter the kitchen. The place was full of smoke and flame and I hit the tiled floor. The Smith-Wesson jerked out my numbed hand and skittered along the polished blocks.

Witherspoon was sagging like a rag doll, his body slammed up against the kitchen cabinet as bright red-rimmed holes were punched in the white shirt. Glass smashed somewhere. He ended his dance by falling forward on his face, small flames lapping the bullet holes until they guttered out into smoky vapour.

I rolled over toward the sink units, watching

the torn vestiges of the paper blind. I got to the Smith-Wesson, loosed off a shot at the window for morale rather than anything else. I crawled back to Witherspoon. There was nothing I could do for him. Nothing anyone could do. He was just another job for the mortician.

I unbolted and went out the kitchen door at a speed that would have astonished Paavo Nurmi in his prime. A dark figure had already gotten to the end of the drive, a mere blur against the flowering hedge. I pounded down anyway, remembering the Buick was parked a long way off.

A car gunned up as I gained the drive entrance. I could hear by the way the engine was revving that the driver was having some problem in backing in order to get out of his parking slot. I remembered then the mass of cars I'd seen earlier.

I still held the Smith-Wesson and I put it back in my pocket, kept my hand on the butt. I ran quickly down the pavement, noting the dark sedan that was clear of the sidewalk now. It went away fast, out the far end of the boulevard. It was too far off now for me to make out either the number plate or the driver.

I sighed. It figured. There was no-one around in the roadway. I put the Smith-Wesson away and went back into Witherspoon's house. I found a phone and put a call through to

164

McGiver. He wasn't at Police H.Q. and I had to get him at home.

I told him who I was and where and why he ought to come on over. I held the phone out from my ear and let the gnat-like buzzings go on until he was all tuckered out.

Then I found a divan in the living room, spread myself, lit a cigarette and sat pasting my tattered nerves together.

CHAPTER NINETEEN

1

It was already dark when I got to Dcirdre Freeman's place. I had only one way to go now. I hadn't taken McGiver entirely into my confidence but I'd given him enough stuff to get myself off the hook and Witherspoon's house was being taken apart by a trained squad.

Not that I thought they'd find anything. My best course was to go head-on at Deirdre Freeman. I still thought it incredible that she could have cut down Jerry Freeman but wives had chilled husbands before for as little as 3,000 dollars, let alone three million.

It seemed like years since I'd first tooled the Buick up the red gravel driveway and parked in front of the Siena-style fountain. There were lights on in the house and I felt the weight of the case, dead and heavy on my heart as I walked up into the colonnaded porch. The white bulk of the mansion sat there, insubstantial in the dim light, like it was waiting to ingest me.

The big front door was still ajar, the lights in the hall shining on the polished parquet floor and gleaming on the smooth balustrades of the spiral staircase. I was about to hit the bell-push when the Filipino maid crossed the hall with a clopping of high heels and saw me standing there in the porch-light. She came forward quickly to greet me, the teeth white in the pale face beneath the black hair.

'Mr Faraday! Good to see you.'

'Good to see you, Adele. Is Mrs Freeman home?'

The girl shook her head, motioning me into the house. As on my last visit she shut the heavy door behind us, sliding the bronze ornament over.

'She had to go out urgently. Her uncle called.'

She lowered her voice like she was afraid we could be overheard.

'It's this awful Red Dragon business. Have you been mixed up in all that, Mr Faraday?'

'Up to my neck,' I said. 'It's what I wanted to see her about.'

I glanced at my watch. It was now around seven-thirty.

'What time did she leave?'

'About half an hour ago,' the girl said. 'Like I told you it seemed pretty urgent.'

'You have the uncle's address?' I said.

An odd expression crossed the maid's face.

'Of course, Mr Faraday. Mr van Dorn lives in a big place off Mulholland Drive. I'll get you the exact location.'

She walked over to a far door and as she opened it and buttoned the light I saw it was got up as a study. I went and stood in the half-open doorway while she rummaged around in the clutter on top of a desk with a red leather top.

'Tell me something, Adele,' I said. 'Now that Mr Freeman's gone, who inherits the property?'

The maid turned a startled face to me. Then she smiled faintly.

'There's no secret about that, Mr Faraday. Miss Deirdre, of course.'

'And is there much money involved? I guess so.'

I waved my hand around to encompass the silent house. There was hestation on the Filipino girl's face now.

'Sure, Mr Faraday. That's no secret either. Lots of money.'

'I'm talking about millions of dollars,' I said.

The girl shrugged. She started walking back toward me with a leather-bound scratchpad in her hand.

167

'So am I, Mr Faraday,' she said quietly. 'Millions of dollars.'

I went on pursuing another train of thought which had suddenly filtered into my mind.

'If Mrs Freeman died too who would inherit?' I said. 'The State of California, I suppose?'

The girl shook her head, tearing off the top sheet of the scratchpad, on which she'd jotted down van Dorn's address.

She pushed the glossy black hair back from her forehead.

'By no means, Mr Faraday. Mrs Freeman's uncle is the sole surviving relative. He gets everything if anything happens to Miss Deirdre, God forbid.'

I absorbed the information in silence, the cogs of my mind meshing firmly now. I wondered why she persisted in addressing a married woman as 'miss'. It sounded like a left-over from the Old South. Except that Adele had probably never been farther south than San Diego.

'You surprise me, Adele.'

The girl shook her head again.

'Not so surprising, really. Though I guess Mr Jerry's murder finally made Miss Deirdre formalise things. She had her lawyer draw up a new will a few days ago.'

'You're giving me a lot of useful information,' I said.

The girl smiled brightly.

168

'That's what I'm here for, Mr Faraday. Mrs Freeman would only tell you the same thing herself. She's the soul of frankness.'

'Like Mr van Dorn?' I said.

The girl smiled again.

'Of course, Mr Faraday. He's a person of the greatest integrity. But then he would be, wouldn't he. A man in his position.'

'In what position?' I said.

The girl's eyes were wide.

'A big businessman like that. President of the Onoco Corporation and all.'

The rest of her sentence was chopped off by the faint breeze. I had a brief impression of her startled face and then I was pounding back toward the Buick as fast as my size nines would take me.

2

I took about half a pound of rubber off the tyres but it was only forty minutes or so later before I drew the Buick to a sliding halt in thick feathers of dust. I left my heap at a junction with Mulholland Drive and walked on down in the warm night, my shadow long and thin in the bloom of the street lamps set atop ornamental copper-sheathed poles.

I guessed it was a private development and if my large-scale was right van Dorn's place should be the fourth property down, at the edge of the bluff. They were big houses here and almost lost in foliage from the road. The palms cut sharp-edged patterns in the dust at my feet as I went on down, the Smith-Wesson making a dead weight on my heart, my breathing shallow, my thoughts angry and confused.

I felt some intangible danger it was hard to put a name to. Not just from the anonymous man in the dark suit who'd tried to kill me the previous night. It may have been him who'd taken out Witherspoon and tried to chop me at the same time but somehow I didn't think so. He'd done a good job, whoever he was. My guess was that the bullet from his gun would match the slugs that had cut short Jerry Freeman's life and that of Lou Harper.

I'd acted pretty dumb on some cases but this beat all. My churning thoughts were interrupted now as I came in sight of the lights of the house I was looking for. It was a Gothic-style mansion, probably built in the late twenties and lovingly restored from what I could see by the light of the fancy lanterns that were set around the grounds on posts at strategic intervals.

I got off the drive as soon as I could. There were a couple of big automobiles out front and I didn't want to advertise my presence. I walked on over turf in the heavy shadow of trees, and skirted the house. I could see more lights now, spilling a fretwork pattern of window bars out on to a long terrace.

170

I went on down, the Smith-Wesson out the holster now, listening to the lonely thumping of my heart, alive to all the faint sounds of the night; the fretting of wind in the trees; the sound of a radio playing far off; a car suddenly back-firing down Mulholland with a detonation that sent my gun-arm jumping.

I eased up in the shadow of a big creeper that swept to the third-storey windows, working out my next move. I didn't know which way to play the situation, or if Deirdre Freeman was even here. She may have already left; but the girl Adele had said van Dorn's summons had been urgent and I figured it would take some time to sort out the situation.

I had all the pieces now but they could be put together two different ways; unless someone broke and gave me a clear lead I could still blow it. Which wouldn't please McGiver who had a lot of ground to cover. I gave myself a brief, sardonic smile in my dim reflection in the dark window-pane of an unlit room I was crouching against.

There was another thing gnawing at the back of my mind. I was pretty exposed out here against the smooth facade of the mansion; though I was in shadow now I should soon have to move on if I wanted to achieve anything tonight. And if the man in the dark suit was still hanging around I should make a prime target.

So I shifted over, little nerves crawling in my

back and in my cheeks. I was in shadow again and close to a big room which had five or six large French windows punched into the facade. Two of them were open and a muffled conversation together with a quantity of cigar smoke was coming from them out into the warm night air.

I went on down, walking softly, a nerve fretting in my cheek. I couldn't see anything through the nearest window because there was a massive piece of furniture blocking my view down the long apartment.

I made it as fast as I could without making any noise, the bulk of the Smith-Wesson pressing against my chest muscles. I could make out the dialogue now. The first voice I caught was a man's, undoubtedly Leo van Dorn's.

'My dear Deirdre, of course, but the whole horrible business is over now.'

Then the low, muffled tones of the girl. I couldn't make out her reply, because she was speaking too quietly.

'Undoubtedly this man Ross,' van Dorn said. 'You ought to get away for a while, put this dreadful affair behind you.'

'I'm sure you're right,' the girl said. 'I feel so low and wretched.'

'That's only natural,' van Dorn said. 'What you need is a little pick-me-up. I have the very thing.'

The big man's shadow moved in the mellow lamplight that was impressed in thin wafers on the tiling at my feet. I flattened myself against the wall, giving my well-known impression of a Virginia creeper as he came to stand, smoking his cigar, not six feet from where I crouched. Then he turned away, so that I could move forward a little to see clearly into the room. Deirdre Freeman sat half in profile to me, on a silk-covered divan at right-angles to a massive stone fireplace. The room was got up very expensively as a drawing room and there was a low log fire burning in the grate for some reason, but I had no time for the decor.

Deirdre Freeman's English style of beauty had never been more pronounced as she sat there, wearing a severe black tailored suit, her silken legs pressed together, her long blonde hair drooping across her eyes as she stared at her uncle.

Leo van Dorn wore a dark formal suit with a chalk stripe, a red wool tie making the only splash of colour against his crisp white shirt. I guessed he'd maybe come straight from his day being President of the Onoco Corporation.

I ducked back as he started to march straight toward me. He was only going to a drinks cabinet against the wall in which the French windows were set and I could see him in profile too as he fussed around with a decanter and glasses, his head turned back as he talked to the girl.

'You'll feel better after this, Deirdre,' he told her. 'I've got something special here that

173

will do wonders for you.'

His tone was casual, quite natural, yet almost too casual. I looked at him sharply, noting the thin glaze of sweat on his forehead. His lips trembled slightly. The movement of his hand was so quick I almost missed it; the small turbulence in the surface of the wine, the momentary clouding of the glass. He put his right hand deep in his jacket pocket before he picked up the silver tray and walked over toward the girl.

He put the tray down on a low coffee table, carefully picking up his own glass first. My suspicions crystallised completely at that moment and everything meshed together.

I stepped out into the middle of the window space, not caring if anyone saw me now, realising that van Dorn had stage-managed everything tonight, even to giving the servants the evening off. Van Dorn held the second glass out to the blonde girl.

'Drink,' he said amiably.

'I shouldn't do that, Deirdre,' I said. 'Unless you want to get dead in a hurry.'

CHAPTER TWENTY

1

There was a sudden crash and fragments of glass mingled with splashes of wine erupted across the parquet. The big man in the dark suit looked stupefied, his jaw sagging.

'Faraday!'

The girl was half up from the divan, the welcome in her eyes mingled with puzzlement. I went quickly to van Dorn, took the girl's glass from his unresisting hand. Fortunately it was only his own drink he'd dropped. I needed the girl's for evidence. I put it down carefully on a big square antique table that was some way off. Then I went to stand between it and Deirdre Freeman's uncle.

He had control of himself again.

'Are you mad, Mr Faraday?'

I shook my head.

'Never more sane, Mr van Dorn.'

I had the Smith-Wesson up now, went over to pat the bulge I'd noticed against the well-cut cloth of his suit. The once affable face turned purple as I tugged the pistol free. He opened his mouth to spit out angry words, thought better of it as I raised the Smith-Wesson.

'I'd like to run some ballistic tests on this,

Mr van Dorn,' I said. 'Just for the record.'

Deirdre Freeman had got up and she came toward me now, her face a mask of astonishment.

'What is all this, Mike? And what are you doing here?'

'It's a long story, Deirdre,' I said. 'And one we can't go into in detail tonight. But it concerns your uncle here.'

The dark flush had died from the big man's face. He was dangerously calm as he turned toward me, all the amiability gone. Even the tan seemed to have been erased from the massive features beneath the silver-grey hair.

'What is all this about death and ballistics tests? My niece and I were just having a quiet drink together.'

'Maybe,' I said. 'And then again maybe not. I'm going to have this pistol checked. Ten to one the slugs will match up. With those of Witherspoon and Harper for sure. And I'm ninety-nine per cent certain that they'll match up with someone else's.'

Van Dorn was a shade paler now but he was keeping his end up fine.

'Have you been drinking, Mr Faraday?'

'You're not convincing anyone,' I said. 'You certainly don't convince me.'

'I don't have to convince you about anything,' he said thickly.

I shrugged.

'That's true. But the police would he

interested. Will be interested. They'll be here as soon as I make the call.'

Van Dorn took one step toward me, a hard, menacing figure now. I held the Smith-Wesson steady on his gut, put his own pistol in my jacket pocket. I was convinced it was the right calibre.

There was a note of desperation in the girl's voice as she broke the heavy silence.

'All this is fantastic, Mike. I don't begin to understand.'

'I'm sure your uncle can explain, Deirdre,' I said. 'What I'm not clear about is why a rich man, head of a great corporation, wants your own personal fortune. I thought he was worth millions too.'

The girl bit her lip, tossing the blonde hair back from her eyes.

'There is something wrong at Onoco, Mike,' she said slowly. 'That's why we had a board meeting. The auditors are in.'

She turned hard eyes on van Dorn.

'Uncle Leo has a very extravagant life-style,' she said with quickening breath.

The big man's face started to crumple and for the first time I saw suspicion crystallise in the girl's eyes.

'It's true that I recently made out my will in my uncle's favour,' she said in clipped tones. 'But what are you suggesting?'

'It should all be easy enough to check now that we have a direction to point in,' I told her.

I gave van Dorn a long look. He was the first to drop his eyes.

'So the Onoco Corporation isn't doing so well. Great organisations have tumbled before. Maybe all that outward dressing on the boulevard back there is a facade.'

There were angry red spots on the big man's cheeks.

'You must be mad, Mr Faraday,' he snapped.

'You already said that,' I told him. 'Let's look at some facts. Your niece asked me to find her husband's murderer. I was looking everywhere but in the right direction. Because you very cleverly planted your own murder in the middle of an unconnected series.'

The girl turned white as she looked at van Dorn. He appeared to flinch away from her momentarily.

'The only thing that linked them was the Red Dragon tattoos,' I said. 'And I was feeding you information because Deirdre must have told you I was on the case. Which was why you were able to put your goons on me so quickly.'

I turned to the girl.

'Your husband loved you,' I said. 'I'm certain there was no-one else, either male or female. That tattoo on his arm wasn't a tattoo at all. It was inked on after his death by a man called Harper who was employed by your uncle here. He was then driven back in the hire-car to where the police found him. That was why you'd never seen the tattoo before.'

The girl had given a little choking cry and turned back to the sagging figure of the man in the dark suit.

'This is a preposterous tissue of lies,' he sneered.

I walked over to the table on which I'd placed the wine glass.

'There's one way to prove it,' I said.

I took the glass back and held it out toward him.

'Drink it,' I said. 'You were going to give it to the girl. If she dies you get the whole fortune.'

Deirdre Freeman was making little choking noises now as she stared incredulously at her uncle. She was scrabbling in her handbag as he backed away.

'No,' he said hoarsely.

I held the glass up to his lips, keeping the Smith-Wesson trained on his gut.

'If it's harmless, drink it,' I said.

The girl's burning eyes were fixed on me now.

'I think you proved your point, Mike,' she said calmly.

Something gleamed in her hand. That was when a boot gritted on the terrace and the whole situation started coming unglued.

The girl was firing so quickly the series of shots seemed like one long explosion. The room was full of smoke and through it the big man in the dark suit who'd appeared in the frame of the open French window suddenly jinked aside. I had the Smith-Wesson up now, aiming for his shoulder. We fired almost simultaneously but he was off balance and distracted and the slug went up in the ceiling, sending plaster raining downward.

The big man spun round as the heavy slug from the Smith-Wesson caught him in the shoulder and went over backward on the terrace. I was on the floor now, my ears deafened by the thunder of the detonations. The front of Leo van Dorn's jacket was a bloody rag, his eyes glazed as he crashed through a bookcase, seemingly nailed there until he started the slow sag toward death.

I kept on rolling, through the French window into the darkness, hearing the hammer clicking on spent shells as Deirdre Freeman went on automatically squeezing the trigger. I had no time for her. I found the gunsel's fallen pistol, put my foot on it. He was moaning in the darkness.

I got over to him; his eyeballs were thin slits of white between the half-closed lids and he screamed as I touched him. I looked at the big hole in his coat from which blood was pumping. It looked pretty bad. I balled my handkerchief, stuffed it in the hole, strapped my belt round him to keep it in position. It was the best I could do.

I picked up the fallen pistol and went through into the big room. Deirdre Freeman was sitting back on the divan, a dazed, frightened figure.

'He deserved to die, Mike,' she said over and over again in a broken voice.

'Sure,' I told her. 'We both know that. We got to make it look right to the police.'

I went over to look at what was left of van Dorn. The damage was worse than I thought. I had an idea then. I guessed the gunsel hadn't seen much when he came in. That van Dorn had had him there was obvious. As extra insurance maybe. Van Dorn couldn't tell me now, that was for sure. And the hood on the terace wouldn't talk even if he lived.

He was a hardened pro who'd been caught in the back-blast of a private quarrel as he came in. It happens sometimes. I went back quickly on to the terrace. I leaned over and examined him. He was already dead. Maybe my slug had caught an artery or something. It had solved one problem. I unbuckled my belt and removed the handkerchief.

I went back inside quickly. The girl had the shakes now. I poured her some brandy from the cabinet, taking it from a bottle on which the seal was unbroken. I forced the yellow stuff between her chattering teeth. She quietened straight away. I had van Dorn's pistol out; I wiped it clean of my prints, pressed the butt into the dead man's right hand. I remembered he'd been right-handed.

Then, using my pen through the trigger guard I positioned it about three feet from the body. The girl watched me with blank eyes.

'That looks about right,' I said.

I stared thoughtfully at the untouched glass on the table. I had no doubt chemical analysis would confirm my theory. A nitro shot, perhaps. That simulated a heart attack and was difficult to trace.

I went and sat next the girl. She suddenly drew closer and clung to me convulsively. The perfume of her hair mingled with the fresh smell of tropical vegetation that was drifting in from the garden outside as we kissed. She pulled gently away from me in the end. I lowered my glance, remembering my unfounded suspicions about her.

'You saved my life,' I said. 'Van Dorn was going to kill me. You got him as I dropped the heavy coming through the window. That's more or less how it happened, anyway. Like you said if anyone needed killing it was your uncle.'

The girl shuddered and drained her glass. I poured her another shot.

'I'll never forget this, Mike,' she said in a husky voice.

'Just remember what I said, honey,' I told her. 'We got to tell the story right. Keep it simple.'

'But will the police buy it?' she said.

I grinned.

'They'll buy anything for a nice tidy case. It's open and shut now. They got the Red Dragon killer. And now they've got another open and shut with the murderer all neatly delivered. We'd better get some law in.

I gave Deirdre the number and told her to get hold of McGiver or leave a message for him. It was better for her to have something to do. I went back out in the garden then, checked the gunsel again. The glint of the sedan beyond the hedge arrested me in midstride.

It hadn't been there before. I went on over, walking in rear, my footsteps crisp in the gravel. I stiffened, breaking out the Smith-Wesson. There was an enormous figure hunched behind the wheel. I stared incredulously, opened the driving door gently.

Big Harry's glazed eyes stared uncomprehendingly into mine. There was still dried blood on the front of his jacket. He must have been made of cast-iron.

'I thought I disposed of you,' I said.

He roused himself then, ignoring the Smith-Wesson barrel.

'My death was exaggerated.'

'You're pretty durable,' I said.

His hammered features relaxed into what was almost an amiable expression.

'You're pretty durable yourself, Faraday.'

'I'd better get you to a doctor,' I said. He shook his head wearily.

'I got patched up temporarily,' he said. 'I won't last the week out. But I got to finish the job.'

'All your friends are dead,' I said. 'Including Mr Big.'

His eyes didn't change expression.

'That's the way it goes sometimes. Who was Mr Big? Just for the record.'

'Guy called Leo van Dorn,' I told him. 'Head of a big corporation who was after a few million dollars more. He employed Mr Rich. He's dead too.'

The giant puckered up his face like the thought processes involved were too difficult to grasp.

'It's a hell of a mess, Mr Faraday. But we're both pros. I want to ask you a favour.'

I looked at him sharply.

'Ask away.'

The huge man turned from the wheel, his breathing shallow and laboured.

'I don't deserve it. But as one pro to another.'

I set fire to a cigarette, holding the Smith-Wesson in my left hand, keeping a wary eye on him.

'I'm listening.'

'I got a girl in Pittsburg,' the big man said through clenched teeth. 'I'd like to visit her again. I'd take it as a great favour if you didn't see me tonight.'

I looked at him carefully. He had the smell of death on him. So far as I was concerned he was irrelevant to the case.

'You'll be lucky to hit Sunset Boulevard,' I said.

The big man gave me a twisted grin.

'That's my business,' he said.

'Tie up some ends for me,' I said.

The big man closed his eyes in pain.

'If I can, Mr Faraday.'

'Why were you on to me so quickly?' I said. 'You had to come from back East.'

Big Harry opened his eyes again.

'We were already here on another job,' he said with the nearest thing I'd seen him give to a smile. 'I don't know the chain of command. We had a phone call from Mr Rich and got your name. We also had to contact Lou Harper and fix the tattoo job.'

Looked like I'd guessed right. I remembered then van Dorn's somewhat abstracted air when I'd first met him at the house. No doubt he'd pumped Deirdre about the unknown visitor. I'd get those final details from her anyway. When we sorted it all out with McGiver.

I stepped back and waved him on.

'Don't get jumping any traffic lights,' I told

him.

The corners of his mouth went up. For a moment he looked almost human. Like I said he was a pro too. I wondered what sort of girl would go for a big ape like that.

'See you in hell,' he said.

I grinned.

'You'll be there before me.'

I stood watching as the big sedan crunched its way down the driveway and on to the boulevard. Maybe he'd make it to Pittsburg. Maybe not. It hardly seemed to matter amid the general carnage.

I turned back to the lemon-yellow squares of the French windows that glowed in the darkness and to the wreckage of the room and the nightmare world that Leo van Dorn and his kind always made.

My brain cogs were turning again; revolving around things that didn't really matter like whether van Dorn had driven the hire-car to the airport to meet Jerry Freeman or if Witherspoon had made the booking. I guessed too that van Dorn had seen me follow Witherspoon through the glass window of his office and had broken off his meeting to drive over to the little man's house in time to shoot him through the blind. Like I said ballistics would prove that for us.

Detail that mattered on the police blotter but some of which was going to be hard to answer now that all the principal witnesses were gone.

I walked toward the window, trying to think of something to say that would be of comfort to Deirdre Freeman; seeing Stella's face floating before me in the velvet darkness; and beyond those images, crowding in, others of violence and death that had bespattered the case from beginning to end.

Shakespeare with the poetry taken out, Stella would have called it. I looked up at the stars, remote and pale and then at the unearthly pall of lights and vapour hanging over the L.A. basin beyond. I gave up beating my brains out and went on in and closed the French doors behind me.